CBSE

[Central Board of Secondary Education]

ENGLISH

CLASS - XII

CONTENT TABLE

Reading Skill	**02 – 10**
Creative Writing Skills	
• Email Writing	11 – 13
• Message Writing	14 – 15
• Paragraph Writing	16 – 18
• Postcard Writing	19 – 20
• Speech Writing	21 – 23
• Debate Writing	24 – 26
• Diary Writing	27 – 28
• Informal Writing	29 - 30
Literature (Flamingo)	
(Prose)	
• The Last Lesson	31 – 32
• Lost Spring	33 – 35
• Deep Water	36 – 37
• The Rattrap	38 – 39
• Indigo	40 – 42
• Poets and Pancakes	43 – 45
• The Interview	46 – 48
• Going Places	49 – 50
(Poetry)	
• My Mother at Sixty-Six	51 – 52
• Keeping Quiet	53 – 54
• A Thing of Beauty	55 – 56
• A Roadside Stand	57 – 59
• Aunt Jennifer's Tigers	60 - 61
Literature (Vistas)	
• The Third Level	62 – 63
• The Tiger King	64 – 66
• Journey to The End of The Earth	67 – 68
• The Enemy	69 – 71
• On the Face of It	72 – 74
• Memories of Childhood	75 - 77

1. Read the passage given below and answer the questions that follow:

To make our life a meaningful one, we need to mind our thoughts, for our thoughts are the foundations, the inspiration and the motivating power of our deeds. We create our entire world the way we think. Thoughts are the causes, and the conditions are the effects. Our circumstances and conditions are not dictated by the world outside; it is the world inside us that creates the outside. Self-awareness comes from the mind, which means the soul. Mind is the sum total of the state of consciousness grouped under thought, will and feeling. Besides self- onsciousness, we have the power to choose and think. Krishna says, "No man resteth a moment inactive." Even when inactive on the bodily plane, we are all the time acting on the thought plane. Therefore, if we observe ourselves, we can easily mould our thoughts. If our thoughts are pure and noble, naturally actions follow the same.

Questions:

(i) How can we make our life meaningful ?

A.	By praying to God	**B.**	By working hard
C.	By minding our thoughts	**D.**	By working for the poor

Ans: C

(ii) What is it that motivates our deeds ?

A.	Our thoughts	**B.**	Our actions
C.	Our surroundings	**D.**	Our relations

Ans: A

(iii) What constitutes our state of consciousness ?

A.	Our thoughts	**B.**	Our will
C.	Our feelings	**D.**	All the above

Ans: D

(iv) How can we mould our thoughts ?

A.	By observing our surroundings	**B.**	By observing our seniors
C.	By observing our juniors	**D.**	By observing our ourselves

Ans: D

(v) According to the passage, what is the role of thoughts in shaping our lives?

A.	Thoughts are the effects of our circumstances and conditions.	**B.**	Thoughts are influenced by the world outside us.
C.	Thoughts are the foundations, inspiration, and motivating power of our deeds.	**D.**	Thoughts are created by self-awareness and the power to choose.

Ans: C

2. Read the passage given below and answer the questions that follow :

People travelling long distances frequently have to decide whether they would prefer to go by land, sea or air. Hardly can any one positively enjoy sitting in a train for more than a few hours. Train compartments soon get cramped and stuffy. It is almost impossible to take your mind off the journey. Reading is only a partial solution, for the monotonous rhythm of the wheels clicking on the rails soon lulls you to sleep. During the day sleep comes in snatches. At night, when you really wish to go to sleep you rarely manage to do so. If you are lucky enough to get a couchette, you spend half the night staring at the small blue light in the ceiling, or fumbling to find your passport when you cross a frontier. Inevitably you arrive at your destination almost exhausted. Long car journeys are even more unpleasant, for it is quite impossible even to read. On motorways you can travel fairly safely at high speeds, but more often than not, the greater part of the journey is spent on narrow, bumpy roads which are crowded with traffic.

Questions:

(i) Why can't a railway passenger enjoy sleep during the day ?

A.	People go on talking.	**B.**	Wheels produce noise.
C.	Sleep comes in snatches.	**D.**	Whistle breaks sleep.

Ans: B

(ii) How does one spend half the night while crossing a frontier ?

A.	Staring at the small red light.	**B.**	Fumbling to find passport.

    C.   Waiting for customs officers.   **D.**   Guarding your goods.

Ans: B

(iii) How does one feel on reaching the destination after a long train journey ?
    A.   Fresh   **B.**   Active
    C.   Smart   **D.**   Exhausted

Ans: D

(iv) How are the long car journeys in comparison to train journeys ?
    A.   Pleasant   **B.**   Risky
    C.   Unpleasant   **D.**   Smoot

Ans: Unpleasant

(v) According to the passage, why are long train journeys often uncomfortable?
    A.   Train compartments are spacious and comfortable.   **B.**   The rhythmic sound of the wheels clicking on the rails can be distracting.
    C.   Train journeys allow for uninterrupted reading and relaxation.   **D.**   Sleeping comfortably is difficult due to cramped conditions and disturbances.

Ans: D

3. Read the passage given below and answer the questions that follow:

Three-fourths of the surface of our planet is covered by the sea, which both separates and unites the various races of mankind. The sea is the great highway along which man may journey at his will, the great road that has no walls or hedges hemming it in, and that nobody has to keep in good repair with the aid of pickaxes and barrels of tar and steamrollers. The sea appeals to man's love of the perilous and the unknown, to his love of conquest, his love of knowledge, and his love of gold. Its green and grey and blue and purple waters call to him and bid him fare forth in quest of fresh fields. Beyond their horizons, he has found danger and death, glory, and gain. In some great continents, such as America and Australia, there are towns and villages many thousands of miles from the coast, whose children have never seen or heard or felt the waves of the sea.

Questions:

(i) How much of our planet is covered by the sea ?
    A.   33 percent   **B.**   50 percent
    C.   75 percent   **D.**   80 percent

Ans: C

(ii) The sea _________ the various races of mankind.
    A.   Separates   **B.**   Unites
    C.   Both (A) and (B)   **D.**   Neither A nor B

Ans: C

(iii) The sea is the great highway _________.
    A.   That man can travel by at his will.   **B.**   That has no walls or hedges.
    C.   That nobody has to keep in good repair.   **D.**   All the above

Ans: B

(iv) In some big continents, children have never seen the sea because _________.
    A.   They live very far away from the sea.   **B.**   They have never heard of the sea.
    C.   They are afraid of the sea.   **D.**   They are poor and have no money to travel.

Ans: A

(v) According to the passage, what are some reasons why the sea appeals to mankind?
    A.   The sea provides a sense of security and protection.   **B.**   The sea offers easy transportation with well-maintained roads.
    C.   The sea represents an opportunity for exploration and conquest.   **D.**   The sea is devoid of any life or resources.

Ans: C

4. Read the passage given below and answer the questions that follow :

New Year is the time for resolution. Mentally, at least most of us could compile formidable lists of 'do's and don'ts'. The same old favourites recur year in and year out with monotonous regularity. We resolve to get-up early each morning, eat healthy food, exercise, be nice to people we don't like and find more time for our parents. Past experience has taught us that certain accomplishments are beyond attainment. If we remain deep rooted liars, it is only because we have so often experienced the frustration that results from failure. Most of us fail in our efforts, at self-improvement because our schemes are too ambitious and we never have time to carry them out. We also 'make the fundamental error of announcing our resolution to everybody so that we look even more foolish when we slip back into our bad old ways. Aware of these pitfalls, this year I attempted to keep my resolutions to myself. I limited myself to two modest ambitions, to do physical exercise every morning and to read more in the evening. An overnight party on New Year's Eve provided me with a good excuse for not carrying out either of these new resolutions on the first day of the year, but on the second, I applied myself diligently to the task. The daily exercise lasted only eleven minutes and I proposed to do them early in the morning before anyone had got up. The self-discipline required to drag myself out of bed eleven minutes earlier than usual was considerable. Nevertheless, I managed to creep down into the living room for two days before anyone found me out. After jumping about on the carpet and twisting the human frame into uncomfortable positions, I sat down at the breakfast table in an exhausted condition. It was this that betrayed me. The next morning the whole family trooped in to watch the performance. That was really unsettling but I fended off the taunts and jibes of the whole family good-humouredly and soon everybody got used to the idea. However, my enthusiasm waned. The time I spent at exercises gradually diminished. Little by little the eleven minutes fell to zero. By January 10th, I was back to where I had started from. I argued that if I spent less time exhausting myself at exercises in the morning, I would keep my mind fresh for reading when I got home from work. Resisting the hypnotising effect of television, I sat, in my room for a few evenings with my eyes glued to a book. One night, however, feeling cold and lonely, I went downstairs and sat in front of the television pretending to read. That proved to be my undoing, for I soon got back to the old bad habit of dozing off in front of the screen. I still haven't given up my resolution to do more reading. In fact, I have just bought a book entitled 'How to Read a Thousand Words a Minute'. Perhaps it will solve my problem, but I just have not had time to read it.

Questions:

(i) What were the writer's two resolutions ?

A. Physical exercise in the morning	**B.** Read more in the evening
C. Both (A) and (B)	**D.** Not to make more resolutions

Ans: C

(ii) How much time did the daily exercise last initially?

A. 10 minutes	**B.** 11 minutes
C. 5 minutes	**D.** 8 minutes

Ans: B

(iii) How many days did the narrator continue his resolution ?

A. 8 days	**B.** 9 days
C. 10 days	**D.** 7 days

Ans: C

(iv) Which book did the narrator buy ?

A. How to read a thousand words a minute	**B.** How to be a good reader
C. How to be firm on your resolutions	**D.** The importance of exercising

Ans: A

(v) According to the writer, past experience of resolutions has taught us:

A. Frustration results from failure.	**B.** Certain accomplishments are beyond attainment.
C. New Year is a time for resolutions.	**D.** Failures are a part of life.

Ans: B

5. Read the following passage given below and answer the questions that follow:

I had submitted an article 'Reforming our education system' recently wherein the need for our educational system to shift its focus from insisting upon remembering to emphasizing or understanding was stressed upon. This article brought back the memory of an interesting conversation between my daughter and myself in the recent times wherein I had learnt that Economics and Physics were a few of the most difficult subjects for her as she had to mug up the answers. Though I offered to help her out with the immediate problem on hand, I learnt subsequently that many a time it pays to mug up the answer properly because the teachers find it easier to evaluate that way. It seems, the more deviation there is from the way the sentences are framed in the textbook, the more risk one runs of losing marks on that count many a time. This reminded me of a training session I had attended at work wherein we were required to carry out an exercise of joining the dots that were drawn in rows of three without lifting the pen and without crossing the trodden path more than once Though the exercise seemed quite simple, almost 95 percent of us failed to achieve the required result, no matter how hard we tried. The instructor then informed us cheerily that it happened all the time, because the dots that appeared to fit into a box like formation do not allow us to think out of the box.

That was when I realised that all of us carry these imaginary boxes in our minds. Thanks to our stereotyped upbringing that forces our thinking to conform to a set pattern. "What is the harm in conforming as long as it is towards setting up a good practice ? someone might want to ask. Perhaps, no harm done to others but to the person being confined to "think by rote" may mean being deprived of rising to the heights he/she is capable of rising to, even without the person being aware of the same. If we instil too much fear of failure in the children right from the young age, the urge to conform and play safe starts stifling the creative urge which dares to explore, err and explore again. As we know, most of the great inventions were initially considered to be most outrageous and highly impractical. It is because the persons inventing the same were not bothered about being ridiculed and were brave enough to think of the unthinkable that these inventions came into being. For many children, studies are the most boring aspect of their lives. Learning, instead of fun is being considered the most mundane and avoidable activity. Thanks to the propagators of an educational system which is more information oriented than knowledge oriented.

Too much of syllabus, too many students per teacher, lack of enough hands-on exercises, teaching as a routine with the aim of completing the syllabus in time rather than with the goal of imparting knowledge, the curriculum more often than not designed keeping in view the most intelligent student rather than the average student are important factors in this regard. Peer pressure, high expectations of the parents in an extremely competitive environment, the multitude of distractions in an era of technological revolution are adding further to the burden on the young minds. For a change, can we have some English/Hindi poems ickle, tickle and pickle the young minds and send them on a wild goose chase for the pot of gold at the end of a rainbow ? Can we have lessons in History that make the child feel proud of his heritage instead of asking him to mug up the years of the events ? Can the physics and chemistry lessons be taught more in the laboratories than in the classrooms ? Can a system be devised so as to make the educational excursions compulsory for schools so that visits to historical/botanical places are ensured without fail ? Can the educational institutes start off inter school projects on the Internet, the way the schools abroad do, so as to encourage the child to explore on her own and sum up her findings in the form of a report ? Finally, can we make the wonder of the childhood last and get carried forward into the adulthood instead of forcing pre-mature adulthood on children ? I, for one, have realised that it is worth doing so, hence I have asked my child to go ahead by choosing to write the answers on her own, in her own language by giving vent to her most fanciful imagination !

Questions:
(i) What were the difficult subjects for the narrator's daughter ?

A.	Biology and Chemistry	**B.**	Economics and Physics
C.	Political Science and English	**D.**	History and Math's

Ans: B

(ii) Why does it pay to mug up answers ?

A.	Because teachers find it easy to evaluate	**B.**	Because students find it easy to write
C.	Because teachers find it easy to teach	**D.**	Because students find it easy to remember

Ans: A

(iii) What stifles the creative urge in children ?

A.	The urge to be always right	**B.**	The urge to do well in everything
C.	The urge to conform and play safe	**D.**	The urge to take risks

Ans: C

(iv) Learning is now being considered ________.

A.	An interesting activity	**B.**	A mundane and avoidable activity
C.	A fun filled activity	**D.**	An interesting but avoidable activity

Ans: B

(v) According to the passage, why does the author emphasize the need for a shift in the educational system?

A.	The author's daughter found Economics and Physics to be difficult subjects.	**B.**	Teachers prefer evaluating answers that are memorized.
C.	The current system stifles creativity and discourages thinking outside the box.	**D.**	The educational system is more focused on information than knowledge.

Ans: C

6. Read the following passage given below and answer the questions that follow :
For four days, I walked through the narrow lanes of the old city, enjoying the romance of being in a city where history still lives –

in its cobblestone streets and people riding asses, carrying vine leaves and palm as they once did during the time of Christ. This is Jerusalem, home to the sacred sites of Christianity, Islam and Judaism. This is the place that houses the church of the Holy Sepulchre, the place where Jesus was finally laid to rest. This is also the site of Christ's crucifixion, burial and resurrection. Built by the Roman Emperor Constantine at the site of an earlier temple to Aphrodite, it is the most venerated Christian shrine in the world. And justifiably so. Here, within the church, are the last five stations of the cross, the 10th station where Jesus was stripped of his clothes, the 11th where he was nailed to the cross, the 12th where he died on the cross, the 13th where the body was removed from the cross, and the 14th, his tomb. For all this weighty tradition, the approach and entrance to the church is nondescript. You have to ask for directions. Even to the devout Christian pilgrims walking along the Via Dolorosa – the Way of Sorrows – first nine stations look clueless. Then a courtyard appears, hemmed in by other buildings and a doorway to one side. This leads to a vast area of huge stone architecture. Immediately inside the entrance, is your first stop. It's the stone of anointing: this is the place, according to Greek tradition, where Christ was removed from the cross. The Roman Catholics, however, believe it to be the spot where Jesus' body was prepared for burial by Joseph. What happened next? Jesus was buried. He was taken to a place outside the city of Jerusalem where other graves existed and there, he was buried in a cave. However, all that is long gone, destroyed by continued attacks and rebuilding; what remains is the massive – and impressive – Rotunda (around building with a dome) that Emperor Constantine built. Under this, and right in the centre of the Rotunda, is the structure that contains the Holy Sepulchre. "How do you know that this is Jesus' tomb?" I asked one of the pilgrims standing next to me. He was clueless, more interested, like the rest of them, in the novelty of it all and in photographing it, than in its history or tradition. At the start of the first century, the place was a disused quarry outside the city walls. According to the gospels, Jesus' crucifixion occurred 'at a place outside the city walls with graves nearby, Archaeologists have discovered tombs from that era, so the site is compatible with the biblical period. The structure at the site is a marble tomb built over the original burial chamber. It has two rooms, and you enter four at a time into the first of these, the Chapel of the Angel. Here the angel is supposed to have sat on a stone to recount Christ's resurrection. A low door made of white marble, partly worn away by pilgrims' hands, leads to a smaller chamber inside. This is the 'room of the tomb', the place where Jesus was buried. We entered in single file. On my right was a large marble slab that covered the original rock bench on which the body of Jesus was laid. A woman knelt and prayed. Her eyes were wet with tears. She pressed her face against the slab to hide them, but it only made it worse.

Questions :
(i) How does Jerusalem still retain the charm of ancient era ?

A.	There are narrow lanes	**B.**	Roads are paved with cobblestones
C.	People can be seen riding asses	**D.**	All of the above

Ans: D

(ii) Holy Sepulchre is sacred to _______.

A.	Christianity	**B.**	Islam
C.	Judaism	**D.**	Both (A) and (B)

Ans: D

(iii) Why does one have to constantly ask for directions to the church ?

A.	Its lanes are narrow	**B.**	Entrance to the church is nondescript
C.	People are not tourist friendly	**D.**	Everyone is lost in enjoying the romance of the place

Ans: B

(iv) Where was Jesus buried ?

A.	In a cave	**B.**	At a place outside the city
C.	In the Holy Sepulchre	**D.**	Both (A)and (B)

Ans: C

(v) Where is the church of the Holy Sepulchre located?

A.	In Jerusalem's old city	**B.**	Outside the city walls of Jerusalem
C.	In a disused quarry	**D.**	Along the Via Dolorosa

Ans: A

7. Read the following passage given below and answer the questions that follow :
We often make all things around us the way we want them. Even during our pilgrimages, we have begun to look for whatever makes our heart happy, gives comfort to our body and peace to the mind. It is as if external solutions will fulfil our needs, and we do not want to make any special efforts even in our spiritual search. Our mind is resourceful - it works to find shortcuts in simple and easy ways. Even pilgrimages have been converted into tourism opportunities. Instead, we must awaken our conscience and souls and understand the truth. Let us not tamper with either our own nature or that of the Supreme. All our cleverness is

rendered ineffective when nature performs a dance of destruction. Its fury can and will wash away all imperfections. Indian culture, based on Vedic treatises, assists in human evolution, but we are now using our entire energy in distorting these traditions according to our convenience instead of making efforts to make ourselves worthy of them. The irony is that humans are not even aware of the complacent attitude they have allowed themselves to sink to. Nature is everyone's Amma and her fierce blows will sooner or later corner us and force us to understand this truth. Earlier, pilgrimages to places of spiritual significance were rituals that were undertaken when people became free from their worldly duties. Even now some seekers take up this pious religious journey as a path to peace and knowledge. Anyone travelling with this attitude feels and travels with only a few essential items that his body can carry. Pilgrims traditionally travelled light, on foot, eating light, dried chickpeas and fruits, or whatever was available. Pilgrims of olden days did not feel the need to stay in special AC bedrooms, or travel by luxury cars or indulge themselves with delicious food and savouries. Pilgrims traditionally moved ahead, creating a feeling of belonging towards all, conveying a message of brotherhood among all they came across whether in small caves, ashrams or local settlements. They received the blessings and congregations of yogis and mahatmas in return while conducting the dharma of their pilgrimage. A pilgrimage is like penance or sadhana to stay near nature and to experience a feeling of oneness with it, to keep the body healthy and fulfilled with the amount of food, while seeking freedom from attachments and yet remaining happy while staying away from relatives and associates. This is how a pilgrimage should be rather than making it like a picnic by taking a large group along and living in comfort, packing in entertainment, and tampering with environment. What is worse is giving a boost to the ego of having had a special darshan. Now alms are distributed, charity done while they brag about their spiritual experiences! We must embark on our spiritual journey by first understanding the grace and significance of a pilgrimage and following it up with the prescribed rules and rituals – this is what translates into the ultimate and beautiful medium of spiritual evolution. There is no justification for tampering with nature. A pilgrimage is symbolic of contemplation and meditation and acceptance, and is a metaphor for the constant growth or movement and love for nature that we should hold in our hearts. This is the truth!

Questions:
(i) How can a pilgrim keep his body healthy ?

A.	By travelling light	**B.**	By eating small amounts of food
C.	By keeping free from attachments	**D.**	Both (A) and (B)

Ans: C

(ii) How do we satisfy our ego ?

A.	By having a special darshan	**B.**	By distributing alms
C.	By treating it like a picnic	**D.**	Both (A) and (B)

Ans: D

(iii) Who is referred to as 'everyone's Amma' in this passage ?

A.	Humans	**B.**	Animals
C.	Nature	**D.**	Insects

Ans: C

(iv) What have been converted into tourism opportunities ?

A.	Pilgrimages	**B.**	Temples
C.	Gurudwaras	**D.**	Churches

Ans: A

(v) According to the passage, what should a pilgrimage primarily be focused on?

A.	Indulging in delicious food and savories	**B.**	Taking a large group along for entertainment
C.	Bragging about spiritual experiences	**D.**	Contemplation, meditation, and acceptance

Ans: D

8. Read the passage given below and answer the questions that follow:
Pollution has been defined as the addition of any substance or form of energy to the environment at a rate faster than the environment can accommodate its dispersion, breakdown, recycling or storage in some harmless form. In simpler terms, pollution means the poisoning of the environment by man. Pollution has accompanied mankind ever since large groups of people settled down in one place for a long time. It was not a serious problem during primitive times when there was more than ample space available for each individual or group. As the human population boomed, pollution became a major problem and has remained as one ever since. Cities of ancient times were often unhealthy places, fouled by human wastes and debris. Such unsanitary conditions favoured the outbreak of diseases that killed or maimed many people living in those times. The rapid advancement of technology and industrialization today is something that man can be proud of. However, it has brought along with it many undesirable results, one of which is the pollution of our environment. Humanity today is threatened by the dangers of air, water, land and noise pollution. The air that we breathe is heavily polluted with toxic gases, chemicals and dust. These consist of the discharge

from industrial factories and motor vehicles. The emission of tetraethyl lead and carbon monoxide from exhaust fumes is a major cause for concern too. Outdoor burning of trash and forest fires has also contributed to air pollution. They cause the smarting of the eyes, bouts of coughing and respiratory problems. Owing to the burning of fossil fuels, the level of carbon monoxide in the air is more than desirable. Too high a level of carbon dioxide will cause the Earth's temperature to rise. The heat will melt the polar caps, thus raising the sea level and causing massive floods around the world. The burning of fuels also produces gases which form acid rain. Acid rain has a damaging effect on water, forest and soil, and is harmful to our health. Man has reached the moon and invented supersonic crafts that can travel faster than the speed of sound. However, these inventions emit pollutants which contribute to the depletion of the ozone layer. This depletion of ozone, which absorbs the harmful rays of sun and prevents them from reaching the Earth, will have drastic effects on all living things. It will lead to a rise in the number of people suffering from skin cancer. Water pollution has become widespread too. Toxic waste has found its way into our lakes, streams, rivers and oceAns: This waste is released by factories and sea going vessels. Spillage of oil by tankers during the recent Gulf War has caused irreparable damage to marine life. Thousands of sea animals have died or were poisoned by the pollutants in their natural habitat. As such, it is dangerous for humans to consume sea food caught in polluted waters. Dumping of used cars, cans, bottles, plastic items and all other kinds of waste material is an eyesore. Much of the refuse is not biodegradable and this interferes with the natural breakdown process of converting substance from a harmful form to a non harmful one. As such, it becomes a hazard to one's health. We are often faced with noises from construction sites, jet planes and traffic jam. We may be unaware of it but noise pollution has been attributed to causing a loss of hearing, mental disturbances and poor performance at work. To control environmental pollution, substances which are hazardous and can destroy life must not be allowed to escape into the environment. This calls for united decision making among the world leaders and a public awareness of the dangers of pollution.

Questions:
(i) Pollution was not a serious problem in ancient times because :

A.	People were unsettled	**B.**	Lot of space was available
C.	Population was less	**D.**	All of the above

Ans: B

(ii) Acid rain does not cause:

A.	Smarting of eyes	**B.**	Water pollution
C.	Soil pollution	**D.**	Damage to forest

Ans: A

(iii) The number of people suffering from skin cancer will rise because :

A.	Man has invented supersonic aircraft's	**B.**	Ozone layer is depleting
C.	No efforts are being made to repair the ozone layer	**D.**	Inventions emit pollutants that deplete the ozone layer which absorbs the cancer causing rays

Ans: B

(iv) If the refuse is not biodegradable, it :

A.	Becomes an eyesore	**B.**	Interferes with natural breakdown
C.	Remains a health hazard	**D.**	Both (A) and (B)

Ans: A

(v) What is one of the undesirable results brought about by rapid technological advancement and industrialization mentioned in the passage?

A.	Increase in the population of marine life	**B.**	Depletion of the ozone layer
C.	Decrease in the number of forest fires	**D.**	Reduction in air pollution levels

Ans: B

9. Read the passage given below and answer the questions that follow:
"It is impossible to think about the welfare of the world unless the condition of women is improved. It is impossible for a bird to fly on only one wing." – Swami Vivekananda

Women are not born, but made. What is better than India to exemplify this statement by Simone de Beauvoir. With the whole world celebrating International Women's Day with great pomp and show, it would be only apt to analyse the position and space Indian women occupy today, and comparing it to the times 60 years ago when the country had just gained independence. With the women participating in nationalist movements to being pushed into domestic household place, to their resurgence as the super-women today, women in our country have seen it all. There have been innumerable debates about gender in India over the years. Much of it includes women's position in society, their education, health, economic position, gender equality, etc. What one can conclude from such discussions is that women have always held a certain paradoxical position in our developing country. On the one hand, the country has seen an increased percentage of literacy among women, and women are allowed to enter into professional fields, while on the other hand the practices of female infanticide, poor health conditions and lack of education still persist.

Even the patriarchal ideology of the home being a woman's real domain and marriage being her ultimate destiny hasn't changed much. The matrimonial advertisements, demanding girls of the same caste, with fair skin and slim figure, or the much criticized fair and lovely ads, are indicators of the slow changing social mores. If one looks at the status of women then and now, one has to look at two sides of the coin; one side which is promising, and one side which is bleak. When our country got its independence, the participation of women nationalists was widely acknowledged. When the Indian Constitution was formulated, it granted equal rights to women, considering them legal citizens of the country and as an equal to men in terms of freedom and opportunity. The sex ratio of women at that time was slightly better than what it is today, standing at 945 females per 1000 males. Yet the conditions of women screamed a different reality. They were relegated to their households, and made to submit to the male-dominated society, as has always been prevalent in our country. Indian women, who fought as an equal to men in the nationalist struggle, were not given that free public space anymore. They became homemakers, and were mainly meant to build a strong home to support their men who were to build the new independent country. Women were reduced to being secondary citizens. The national female literacy rate was an alarmingly low 8.9 percent. The Gross Enrollment Ratio (GER) for girls was 24.8 percent at primary level and 4.6 percent at the upper primary level (in the 11 – 14 years age group). There existed insoluble social and cultural barriers to education of women and access to organised schooling.

Questions :
(i) The writer says that the women have seen it all because :

A. They participated in the nationalist movements.	**B.** They were pushed into household space.
C. They have become superwomen today.	**D.** All of the above.

Ans: D

(ii) Pick one statement which brings out the paradoxical nature of women's position in society today :

A. They are entering professional fields and becoming literate.	**B.** They lack education and female infanticide is still rampant.
C. They are still victims of patriarchal mindset.	**D.** While they are allowed to enter professional fields they are still victims of patriarchal mindsets.

Ans: D

(iii) The Indian Constitution did not ensure :

A. That women get equal rights.	**B.** That they were considered equal to men.
C. That the sex ratio would be 945 females to 1000 males.	**D.** That they were legal citizens of india.

Ans: A

(iv) Despite the provisions of the constitution :

A. Women were relegated to the household.	**B.** Women were not allowed free space.
C. Women were dictated by patriarchy.	**D.** All of the above.

Ans: D

(v) What was the position of women in India immediately after gaining independence?

A. Women were actively participating in nationalist movements.	**B.** Women had equal rights and opportunities as men.
C. Women were primarily confined to domestic households.	**D.** Women had a high literacy rate and access to education.

Ans: C

10. Read the passage given below and answer the questions that follow :
Russia in the late nineteenth and early twentieth centuries was a massive empire, stretching from Poland to the Pacific, and home in 1914 to 165 million people of many languages, religions and cultures. Ruling such a massive state was difficult, and the long term problems within Russia were eroding the Romanov monarchy. In 1917 this decay finally produced a revolution which swept the old system away. Several key fault lines can be identified as long term causes, while the short term trigger is accepted as being World War – I. It's important to remember Tsarist Russia collapsed under its own flaws, with the top rending, not by an attack from people at the bottom, e.g. workers. That (and Lenin) would come later in 1917, when the Tsar was gone. The revolution was also not inevitable: the Tsars could have reformed, but the last ones didn't want to and went backwards. It cost them their lives. In theory their life had improved in 1861, before which they were serfs who were owned and could be traded by their landowners. The year 1861 saw the serfs freed and issued with small amounts of land, but in return they had to pay back a sum to the

government, and the result was a mass of small farms deeply in debt. The state of agriculture in Russia was poor, using techniques deeply out of date and with little hope of improving thanks to the widespread illiteracy and no capital to invest. Families lived just above the subsistence level, and around 50% of the families had a member who had left the village to find other work, often in the towns.

As the central Russian population boomed, land became scarce. Their life was in sharp contrast to the rich landowners, who held 20% of the land in large estates and were often members of the Russian upper class. The western and southern reaches of the massive Russian Empire were slightly different, with a larger number of better off peasants and large commercial farms. The result was, by 1917, a central mass of disaffected peasants were angry at increased attempts to control them, and at people who profited from the land without directly working on it.

The common peasant mindset was firmly against developments outside the village, and desired autonomy. Oddly, although the vast majority of Russia in population was rural peasants, and urban expeasants, the upper and the middle classes knew little of real peasant life, but a lot about myths: of down to earth, angelic, pure commercial life, etc. Legally, culturally, socially, the peasants in over half a million settlements were organised by centuries of community rule, the mirs, which were separate from elites and the middle class. But this was not a joyous, lawful commune, it was a desperate struggling system fuelled with the human weakness of rivalry, violence and theft, and everywhere was run by elder patriarchs. A break was occurring among the peasants between the elders and a large number of young literate peasants, due to the culture of deeply ingrained and frequent violence. The peasants were not without a world view, and it was a mixture of odd folk memory, custom, and opposition to the interference of the Tsar – Inside vs outside. Stolypin's lands reforms of the years before 1917 attacked peasant concept of family ownership and tried to capitalise it; revolutionary peasants often went back to communal systems. This wasn't so much class but a view based on justice of poor vs strong. In central Russia, the peasant population was rising and land was running out, so eyes were on the elites who were forcing the debt ridden peasants to sell land for commercial use. Even more peasants travelled to the cities in search of work. There they urbanised and looked negatively on the peasants left behind.

Questions :
(i) The decay that caused the Russian revolution was due to :

A. Massive empire	**B.** Failure of the czars to reform themselves
C. World war-i	**D.** All of the above

Ans: D

(ii) The agriculture was in bad condition as :

A. Farmers were in debt	**B.** Techniques were outdated
C. Both (A) and (B)	**D.** Serfs could be traded by their landowners

Ans: C

(iii) Which of the following was the trigger for the revolution ?

A. World War – I	**B.** Urbanisation of the peasants
C. Break between the elders and the young	**D.** Excessive control of the upper classes

Ans: C

(iv) The peasants were organised into communes by :

A. Mirs	**B.** Farmers
C. Middle classes	**D.** Elites

Ans: A

(v) What was one of the long-term causes of the revolution in Tsarist Russia?

A. Urbanization and migration of peasants to cities.	**B.** The lack of reforms by the Tsars.
C. Poor agricultural techniques and widespread illiteracy.	**D.** Land scarcity and increased attempts to control peasants.

Ans: D

Email Writing

Email writing

An email is a method of composing, sending, storing, and receiving messages over an electronic communication system. Here we have discussed what is formal and informal email. The method for formal email has been discussed in detail here (stepwise). The students can see how to compose a formal email and practice writing following the method and email format given below.

Email stands for electronic mail. It is the most preferred means of communication because it is cheaper and faster.

Emails are of three types

- Semi-Formal email
- Informal email
- Formal email

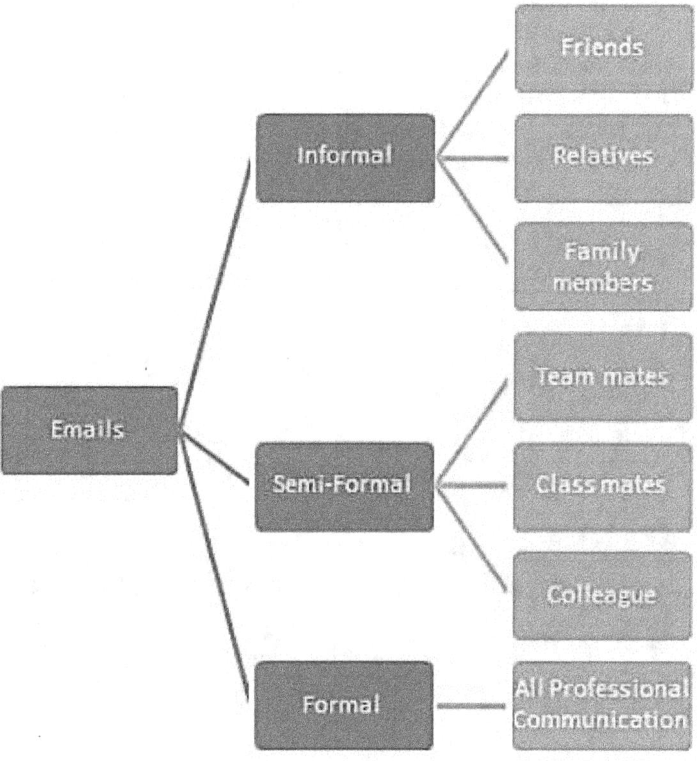

Semi-formal email

An email written for a colleague or a team-mate within a project comes under this category. The language used is simple, friendly, and casual. Modesty and dignity must be maintained.

Informal email

An informal email is written to any relatives, family, or friends. There are no particular rules for informal email writing. A person can use any language of his or her choice.

Formal email

Suppose we are writing or composing an email for any type of business communication. It will come under the category of formal email. Formal email writing will be an email written to companies, government departments, school authorities or any other officers.

Advantages of email writing

- It provides a written record of the communication.

- Email writing is an instantaneous form of communication.
- It can be used anytime and anywhere.
- It is a cheaper form of communication.
- Email helps to contact or send information to a large group of people.

Disadvantages of email writing

- One can get many junk emails
- There is no guarantee if the reader reads the email or not
- The details can be used for identity theft
- We need to have the internet to receive or send emails
- Viruses are easily spread via email attachments

Effective emails

Email writing is a form of expressing ideas or queries. It is helpful only if we write an email in clear and unambiguous terms. Effective email writing has the property of clarity of statement, the needed solution with clear, logical, and simple language. Email writing can be successful if we follow some rules. These are the rules of

- Greeting
- Introduction
- Giving Context or information
- Call for action

Reatures of email:

- There are many features of email. Some of them are as follows
- Automatic reply to messages
- Notification of delivering or not of a message
- Facility to send copies of a message to many people
- Signatures can be attached
- Automatic using the date and time
- Attachments in the form of files, graphics or sound can be sent
- Mobile friendly emails facility
- Auto forward of messages
- The address can be stored in an address book
- The address can be used in the near future
- Automatic filing and retrieval of messages.

Sample

1. Your friend wants to visit Rajasthan. Write an e-mail giving your knowledge about Rajasthan.

Answer:

Date:16/6/20XX:

To: jeevan2000@gmail.com

Cc: mahesh@gmail.com

Subject: Knowledge about Rajasthan Dear Mahesh

Hello! How are you I'm fine here? Last week me and my family went to Rajasthan. It's a
beautiful place. We enjoyed very well. There are many places which should be seen. Thar desert as you know it's the largest desert in India. Royal Palaces and lakes are also worth watching.

Regards

Jeevan

2. Write an e-mail to the supervisor intimating about your absence sign as Jane Doe.

Answer:

Date: 2/3/20XX

To: Joseph 07@gmail.com

Cc: Suzane@ Rediffmail.com

Subject: Jane Doe – Absent from Work Dear Supervisor Joseph

I've got down with the flu and will not be coming in on Tuesday, March 2, so that I can take rest and recover. I've asked Patricia
to check on my clients to ensure all of their needs are met and Tom will prepare the report for our Friday meeting.

I will try and check the email if you need anything urgent. Thank you,

Jane

3. Congratulate your younger brother by email as he has won the first prize in an inter- school debate competition.

Answer:
Date: 28/2/20XX
To: Krishna @gmail.com
Cc: Rupesh@gmail.com
Subject: Congratulation on winning first prize. Dear Krishna
Hearty congratulation!
I was extremely glad to know that you have won the first prize in an inter-school debate competition. I always knew your ability to speak fluently and effectively. It shows you have further sharpened your skill of arguing. You have done pride to all of us in the family. I hope, along with the activities, you will equally perform well in the academic areas.
Love
Rupesh

4. You have just passed out from a school which is now celebrating its annual day. On this occasion, you have been invited to receive a prize for some past activity. Send an email to the principal regretting your inability to attend the function.

Answer:
Date: 4/3/20XX
To: principal@kvjodhpur.com
Cc: Abhishek01@gmail.com
Subject: Inability to attend the function Dear sir,
Kindly accept my heartfelt thanks for inviting me to receive my prize for the first position I had won in a solo song competition in my school days. But I regret to say that I will not be able to come to the Annual day celebration as I have to appear at an entrance exam in an institute that day. I shall come someday to seek your blessings and collect my valued prize.
Regards,
Abhishek

Messages writing

When you were not at home, your friend called and informed your sister about the cancellation of a plan for the next day. So, your sister will leave you a message before going out to inform you about your friend's call.

Messages can be passed through different mediums, be it phones, texts, or emails. But for school students, a generic form of message writing is included under the English syllabus. For this type of writing, they get to learn about retrieving and interpreting information through the conversation given. Then, they are taught about writing the basic inputs into a well- drafted format. Message Writing | Message Writing Format, Examples and How to Write a Message?

February 15, 2021, by Prasanna

Message Writing: A message is a short piece of information given in a written format. When a person cannot speak to another person directly, he/she leaves a hand-written note or forward a text message through mobile or any communicating source. Sometimes the message is also sent orally by voice messages.

The primary concerns of the discussion ought to be fused in the message precisely and plainly. It instructs understudies to recover and decipher data. A message can likewise becomposed dependent on some composed contributions, rather than a telephonic discussion. For example, a declaration or composed notes.

Message writing format:

- HEADING
- DATE
- TIME
- SALUTATIONS
- BODY
- SENDER

The message should be conveyed to another person in a proper format, whether it is a formal or informal message. The message should be written in a polite manner. Informal messages can be written in a casual manner but in an understandable language. The formal message writing will require the below-given format.

- **HEADING–** Message writing begins by writing the word "Message" in bold and capitals. It is written in the middle of the line. This is done in order to catch the attention of the person for whom the message is drafted.
- **DATE–** The date is written on the left-hand side of the page. It is written in expanded form.
- **TIME–** Time can be written both on the left and right sides of the message. However, it is preferable for you to mention it on the right side in order to show a wise usage of space.
- **SALUTATIONS-** Before writing the main content (body) of the message, it is important to address the reader. It helps in avoiding ambiguity and appears to be polite.
- **BODY–** It is the main content of the message wherein you provide all the information that needs to be conveyed to the person you are unable to contact. It is important to stick only to vital information and keep the body of the message short and crisp. Avoid using long sentences.
- **SENDER–** Once you are done with the body of the message, mention your name (or the one given in the question) on the left-hand side of the page. This helps the reader to identify the sender of the message.

Sample

You are Rohit. I received a phone call from Aakash today. You had the following telephonic conversation with Aakash, friends of your elder brother. Write a brief message for your brothers when you will have to go to the playground.

Aakash: Hello, is this 87689546XX?
Rohit: Yes. May I know who's calling?
Aakash: I am Aakash, a friend of Karan. Where is he? Rohit: He has gone to father's office. Can I help you?
Aakash: Oh, sure. Please tell him that he will be taking math notes and geometry box intuition class because tomorrow will be a math test. Could you please give him this message?
Rohit: Okay, I'll give him this message.
Aakash: Thank you.

Ans:
Message
08th March, 20XX 10:00 am
Dear brother

Naksh had called upon you when going to father's office. Today, he had informed me that I would bring math notes and a geometry box to tuition class because tomorrow will be a math test.

Rohit

You are Rajesh, receive a phone call from your father's office Mr. Rahul, when he is absent. Draft the message not more than 50 words following this conversation when you will be going to the library.

Mr. Rahul: Hello, is this 98417854XX?
Rajesh: Yes. May I know who's calling?
Mr. Rahul: I am Rahul Singha. Can I talk to Mr. Agrawal?
Rajesh: Father is not at home. Do you have any messages for them?
Mr. Rahul: Yes, please tell him to come to the office tomorrow at 11 am, there is an urgent meeting with the manager. Could you please give him this message?
Rajesh: Okay, I'll give him this message.
Mr. Rahul: Thank you.

Ans:
Message
17th April, 20XX 10:00 am
Dear father
Mr. Rahul called from your office on the telephone saying that the information tomorrow will be an urgent meeting with the manager at 11 am.

Rajesh

You are Smitha. Your sister is not at home. You received a call from her friend that her dance class got cancelled. Since you are in a rush to go out, so you will leave a message for her. Now write the message with a word limit of fewer than 50 words.

Madhuri: Hello! Is Kavita at home?
Smitha: No. She went outside. May I know who is this calling?
Madhuri: I am Madhuri, Kavita's friend.
Smitha: Ok. Is there any message for her, I can pass?
Madhuri: Yes, please tell her that tomorrow's dance class is cancelled, since our dance teacher had an emergency, and she has to go out of town. The next class will be on Tuesday.
Smitha: Sure. I will let her know. Thank you. Madhuri: You are welcome!

Ans:
Message

Dear Kavita,
Your friend Madhuri called today, and she has informed me that tomorrow's dance class is cancelled, as your dance teacher has to go out of town for some emergency. Your next class will be on Tuesday.

Smitha

You are Ishika, going to tuition class, receiving a phone call from your father's, and told that he would be late and that he would not be able to attend dinner because of an important meeting. Please write a message to inform your mother, who has gone to meet her friend at her house.

Ans:
Message
16th November, 20XX 12:30 pm
Dear mother
The father called to tell him that he would be late from the office due to an important meeting, adding that they would not attend the dinner either.
Ishika.

Paragraph writing

A series of sentences that are organized and coherent and are all related to a single topic is called Paragraph. Breaking the large sentence essay or topic into smaller pieces in a well- structured form is known as Paragraph. The lines that should include in a paragraph is at least three to five, not more. It includes topic sentences, supporting sentences as well as concluding sentences that refer to an overall structure, which is a group of sentences focusing on a single topic.

Paragraphs are the group of sentences combined together, about a certain topic. It is a very important form of writing as we write almost everything in paragraphs, be it an answer, essay, story, emails, etc. We can say that a well-structured paragraph is the essence of good writing. The purposes of the paragraph are to give information, to explain something, to tell a story, and to convince someone that our idea is right.

Paragraphs are blocks of textual content that segment out a larger piece of writing—stories, novels, articles, creative writing, or professional writing portions—making it less complicated to read and understand. Excellent paragraphs are an available writing skill for plenty of types of literature, and proper writers can substantially beautify the clarity of their news, essays, or fiction writing whilst constructing nicely.

Types of paragraphs

There are four types of paragraphs that you need to know about: descriptive, narrative, expository, and persuasive. If you have a quick search on the web then you may found other types too but to make your paragraph simple and succinct, it's a good idea to study just these four.

Having knowledge about what are the type of paragraphs is one of the most essential aspects while writing a paragraph. So, we thought of explaining a bit about paragraph writing types is a must. Okay, let's start about it.

- Descriptive Type of Paragraph: This paragraph type describes the topic and displays the reader what's the subject included in it. The terms selected in the description type usually appeal to the five senses of touch, smell, sight, sound, and taste. This type of paragraph can be more artistic and may vary from grammatical standards.
- Expository Type of Paragraph: It defines something or gives instruction. It may also explain a process and influence the reader step by step via a form of the method. This Expository Para usually needs research, but also, it's possible to rely on the writer's own knowledge and experience.
- Narrative Type of Paragraph: In simple words, this type of paragraph narrates a story that includes a sequence of topic sentences like a clear start, middle of the topic, an end to the paragraph.
- Persuasive Type of Paragraph: This kind of paragraph seeks to make the audience to admit a writer's point of view or know his/her position. Persuasive paragraphs are often used by the teachers because it is beneficial when building an argument. Also, it makes a writer to research and collects some facts on the topic.

Parts of a paragraph

The basic paragraph consists of three parts: a topic sentence, supporting details, and a concluding sentence. This basic paragraph format will help you to write and organize one paragraph and transition to the next.

Concluding sentence

It is the end of the paragraph which is also known as final statement about the topic. It ties all ideas given in the paragraph and emphasizes the main idea one last time. In the concluding sentence, the writer usually restates their topic sentence or summarizes the main points of the paragraph.

Topic sentence

Often, the Topic sentence is the first sentence of a paragraph. Also, we can call an introduction sentence of a paragraph. It states the main idea of each paragraph and displays how the idea connects to the thesis or overall focus of the paper. All consequent points presented in the paragraphs must support the topic sentence.

Supporting details

The supporting sentences explain more about the topic sentence by showing some facts, stats, or examples regarding the topic. It also includes the writer's experience & own analysis and used to develop the topic sentence. The following are common origins of supporting details:

Expert opinion
- Facts and Statistics
- Personal Experiences
- Others' Experiences
- Brief Stories
- Research Studies
- Your Own Analysis
- Interviews

Sample
Write a descriptive paragraph on Coronavirus (COVID-19) within 150 to 200 words.

Paragraph on coronavirus (covid-19)

The name "coronavirus" is derived from Latin "corona", meaning "crown" or "wreath", itself a borrowing from Greek "korone", "garland, wreath". Corona viruses are a group of related RNA viruses that cause respiratory tract infection disease in humans. On December 2019, in Wuhan, China the outbreak was traced to a novel strain of coronavirus, which was given the interim name 2019-nCoV by the World Health Organisation (WHO). Coronavirus disease (COVID-19) is an infectious disease caused by a newly discovered coronavirus. The COVID-19 virus spreads primarily through droplets of saliva or discharge from the nose when an infected person coughs or sneezes. COVID-19 affects different people in different ways. Most infected people will develop mild to moderate illness and recover without hospitalization. Most common symptoms are fever, dry cough, tiredness. Less common symptoms are aches and pains, sore throat, diarrhoea, conjunctivitis, headache, loss of taste or smell, a rash on skin, or discolouration of fingers or toes. Serious symptoms are difficulty breathing or shortness of breath, chest pain or pressure, loss of speech or movement. To prevent infection and to slow transmission of COVID-19, one should wash his hands regularly with soap and water, or clean them with alcohol-based hand rub, maintain at least 1 metre distance between oneself and people coughing or sneezing, avoid touching face, cover mouth and nose when coughing or sneezing, stay home if one feels unwell, refrain from smoking and other activities that weaken the lungs and practice social distancing.

Write a descriptive paragraph on THE IMPORTANCE OF TREES / MAN AND TREES / AFFORESTATION within 150 to 200 words

The importance of trees

Trees are useful and beautiful gifts of nature. Forests help in maintaining the ecological balance' which is so essential for preservation of life on this earth. Existence of man on earth, therefore, depends on forests. Forests provide immense wealth and riches for us. They yield timber and fuel wood, bamb0os, canes, leaves, fruit, fibers, and grasses. The other useful products from forests are shellac, resins. precious herbs and medicinal plants.

They are also great sources oi material for paper, rubber, and gums. Forests have a direct influence on the climate of a region. They induce rains and prevent air pollution. An area devoid of forests will go barren and turn out to be a desert in course of time. The roots of trees bind loose soil and thus help in soil conservation". The top fertile soil is thus retained which is so vital for agriculture. Arrest of soil erosion also prevents silting and raising of riverbeds and possible overflowing of rivers causing floods. Forests protect us from inclement wind also. With increase in population and rapid industrialization, random deforestation has taken place. This has resulted in dwindling" rainfall, depletion in ground water level and Occurrence of droughts', Forests are nature's most precious gilts which feed us physically an aesthetically. They constitute the resource reservoir for human welfare and their management should be planned on a global level. The socioeconomic pattern of a particular continent or a country does get perceptibly influenced by forests. Indiscriminate felling of trees this depletes the forest wealth beyond redemption. The rehabilition of forests and maintenance of proper forest cover and ecosystem are therefore the only way left to us or our survival.

Write a descriptive paragraph on VALUE OF SPORTS / PHYSICAL EXERCISE / THE NECESSITY OF PHYSICAL FITNESS within 150 to 200 words.

Value of sports

The word SPORT stands for sincerity, punctuality, obedience, regularity, and tenacity. These are all essential qualities of a person to do well in life. The proverb runs-"All work and no play make Jack a dull boy. The strain of work and the monotony of the daily routine tire our body and mind. It tells upon our nerves. The sports can refresh them and supply fresh vigour to our body and mind. Hence there 1S a Latin proverb "men's sane in compression", that is 'a sound mind in a sound body. On the contrary, a diseased body makes a mind diseased. So good health is most important in our life. We must remember that wealth or education 1S of little use to a person of ill health. So physical exercise is a must. But it varies according to age and sex of an individual. There are various kinds of sports and exercises like swimming. boating, running. jumping and games like football, cricket, hockey, tennis, badminton, volleyball, basketball, and exercises with the help of instruments etc. Everyone Can select a sport out his own choice and take part init. But what is important to know is that what is necessary and good for a particular manor woman may not be suitable and even may be harmful for another. In this respect advice of an expert in physical education is quite useful. So, there are physical instructors in schools and colleges to guide the students as we know the choice depends on age, ability, and opportunity for taking a particular physical Exercise. However, we must note that time and space never stand in the way or physical exercise, as walking and deep breathing are also good exercises. A few minutes and a small open space are enough for it. So, none need stand aloof. We 'should keep in mind that nutrition, healthy habits and disciplined life are essential for physical fitness. Sports have a great significance in our individual as well as our collective life. It builds our body and gives us more energy in work. It gives us skill., discipline, sense of co-operation and team spirit. Some games call forth courage and presence of mind. Sports and games are joyful activities to0. A true sportsman is frank, generous, and free from petty spite. These are sportsman-like qualities. Of course, Over- exercise is often more harmful than no exercise However, we should keep in mind that regularity must be maintained in physical exercises as it is the mainspring for getting any benefit from any physical exercise.

Write a descriptive paragraph on Global Warming: A Threat within 150 to 200 words.

Global warming: a threat

Global warming means the increase in the average temperature of the earth's surface and oceans. his 1S caused by the gradual increase of greenhouse gases like carbon dioxide and methane in the atmosphere. These gases prevent the heat on the earth's surface from escaping into space. As a result, the glaciers around the world have started melting. The ice in Antarctica is also melting very rapidly. The level of water in the oceans is steadily increasing. This threatens to wipe out many islands and coastal regions. Cities and towns situated near the rivers may be flooded completely. It is thought that the Gangotri glacier, the source of the river Ganga, would melt completely in the next fifty years. The water level of the Ganga will rise by several meters endangering all the cities and towns situated on its banks. Measures to reduce the emission of greenhouse gases should be taken immediately prevent a global crisis.

Postcard writing

Postcards are convenient for sending brief messages, acknowledging receipt of letters and goods or for confirming some engagement already fixed. For a longer/private message, either an inland letter or an envelope is used. Postcards are written in the same manner as letters. Hance the heading, the subscription and the name of the sender are essential in addition to the 'message' and the name and address of the Addressee. Postcards are written in the same manner as an informal letter is written.

Important points while writing a postcard:

- The place and date are written in the same line.
- The sender's complete address is not written.
- The salutation, subscription, and sender's name must be written.
- Write the address of addressee in the appropriate space.

Front side

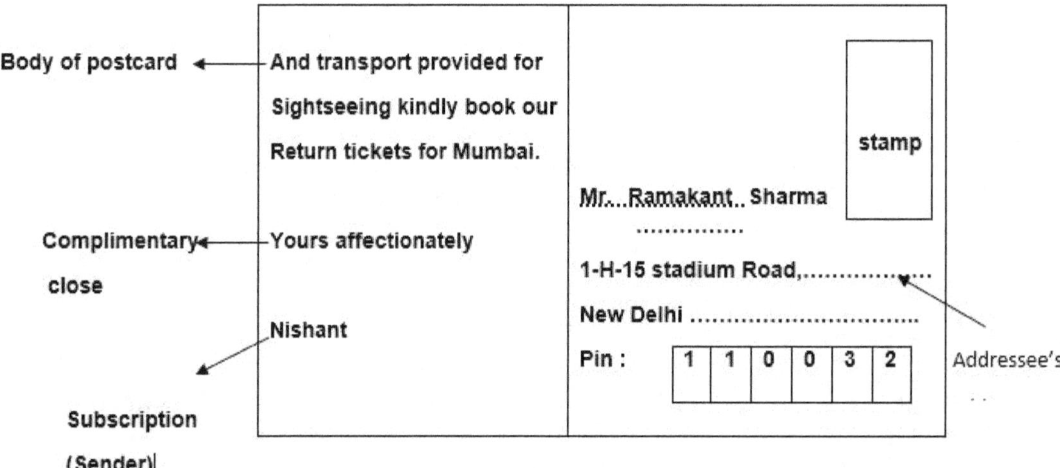

Back side

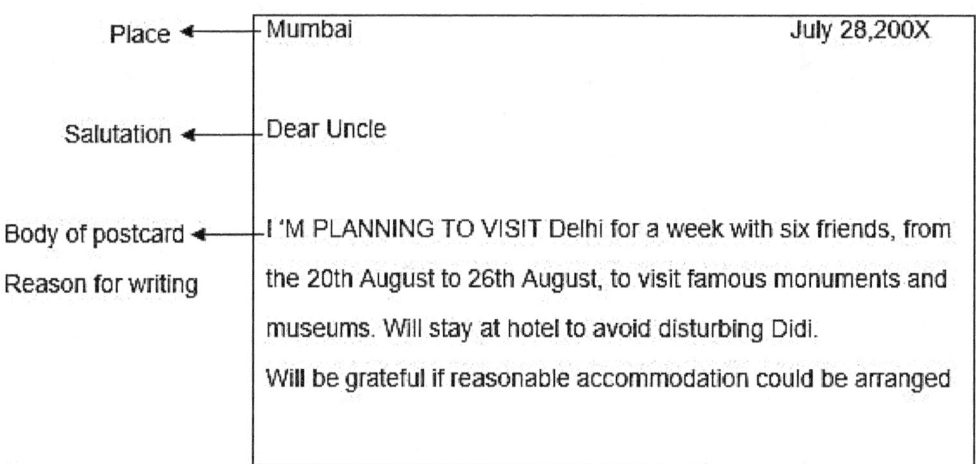

Sample

Write a postcard to your father for his permission to go on an education tour.

Ans:

Netaji Hostel
Kendriya Vidyalaya
Kolkata
4.9.2014

My dear Father

Our class teacher has arranged an education tour. The students of the class can avail this opportunity to go to Delhi and other places. I want to join this tour. Please send me your permission and the money for this purpose.

<table>
<tr><td>

I will need Rs. 2000/- (Rupees

two thousand only). Kindly send

the money also.

Yours lovingly

Mrinal

</td><td>

To

Mr M.K. Sane

23, Nandigram

West Bengal

</td></tr>
</table>

Anupam Verma was on his way to a round tour of south India with his school party. At Sonepat, just before the Jhelum Express was due to arrive, he remembered something important It was that he issued a cheque for his friend, but he left it in his coat's pocket. His friend was to collect it after 3 days and he was to ask his mother to give that to his friend. He decided to write a postcard to his brother, Arun, asking him to give thecheque to his friend when he called. He had only a few minutes before his train left. Write the postcard to Aran, using not more than 50 words.

Answer:

20 June 2016

Dear Arun

I forgot to ask you

<table>
<tr><td>

Your brother

Anupam Verma

</td><td>

MR ARUN VERMA

1250, SECTOR 14

SONEPAT (HARYANA)

</td></tr>
</table>

Puran Singh is to board the Shatabdi Express on way to Kolkata. At New Delhi railway station, just before the train is going to leave the station, he remembers that he has put the keys of the almirah among his books. He decides to write a postcard to his sister Sonu asking her to put the keys either at the mantelpiece or give them to mother. Write the postcard to Sonu, using not more than 50 words.

Answer:

15 March 2017

Dear Sonu

Now it is just 5 minutes for the train to leave. I suddenly remember that I left the almirah keys among my books. Please put them on the mantelpiece. Alternatively, you may give them to mother to avoid.

<table>
<tr><td>

unnecessary trouble.

Your brother

Puran Singh

</td><td>

MS SONU

6, VASANT KUNJ

NEW DELHI

</td></tr>
</table>

Speech Writing

Speech Writing:

A speech is an effective way of communicating a message to a large audience. It is one of the ways of spreading awareness regarding social issues or giving information regarding other important issues. As a form of writing a speech is similar to an article except that it begins with a formal address to the audience, is more conversational in tone and concludes with a 'Thank you'. A speech is written for a specific purpose like informing, persuading, convincing or entertaining an audience.

Types of Speeches

Speeches can be divided into the following categories: the informative speech, the persuasive speech, and speeches for special occasions.

Informative Speech

If the speech's purpose is to define, explain, describe, or demonstrate, it is an informative speech. The goal of an informative speech is to provide information completely and clearly so that the audience understands the message. Examples of informative speeches include describing the life cycle stages of an egg to a chicken, explaining how to operate a camera, or demonstrating how to cook a side dish for a meal. The organization of the speech depends on your specific purpose and varies depending on whether you are defining, explaining, describing, or demonstrating. Informative demonstration speeches lend themselves well to the use of visual aids to show the step-by-step processes with real objects.

Persuasive Speech

Persuasive speeches are given to reinforce people's beliefs about a topic, to change their beliefs about a topic, or to move them to act. When speaking persuasively, directly state near the beginning of the speech what is good or bad and why you think so. This is your thesis statement, which you should give early in the speech. One way to structure a persuasive speech is to use the five-part argument:

- The introduction attracts the attention of the audience, sets the tone, and describes what the persuasive speech is about. The introduction usually includes the thesis statement—the specific sentence that explains the main point of the argument.
- The background provides the context and details needed for a listener to understand the situation being described, as well as the problem or opportunity being addressed.
- Lines of argument make up the body of the speech. Here is where you include all your claims, reasons, and supporting evidence that help make your points effectively.
- Refuting objections means disproving, ruling out, and countering any potential objections before the listeners can think of reasons not to be persuaded.
- The conclusion is where you present your closing arguments. To be effective, the conclusion should restate your thesis statement and summarize the main points of your argument. If you are advocating a particular solution to a problem or a decision to be made, you should close by asking your listeners to adopt your point of view.

Format of Speech Writing

Introduction: Greet the audience, tell them about yourself and further introduce the topic.

Body: Present the topic in an elaborate way, explaining its key features, pros and cons, if any and the like.

Conclusion: Summary of your speech, wrap up the topic and leave your audience with a compelling reminder to think about!

Let's further understand each element of the format of Speech Writing in further detail:

Introduction

After the greetings, the introduction is essential to assure your listeners that you have something productive to say. The introduction must effectively include:

- A brief preview of your topic.
- Define the outlines of your speech. (For example, I'll be talking about ...First ..Second ...Third)
- Begin with a story, quote, fact, joke, or an observation in the room. It shouldn't be longer than 3-4 lines. (For Example: "Mahatma Gandhi said once…", or "This topic reminds me of an incident/story…")

This part is also important because that's when your audience decides if the speech is worth their time. Keep your introduction factual, interesting, and convincing.

Body

Your body consists of all the main points your speech is about. Prepare a flow chart of the details in a systematic way.

For example: If your speech is about waste management; distribute information and arrange it according to subparagraphs for your reference. It could include:

- What is Waste Management?
- Major techniques used to manage waste

- Advantages of Waste management
- Importance of Waste management

If you are speaking about advantages and briefly switching between points, it makes your speech look unorganized and confuses your audience.

Conclusion

The conclusion should be something that the audience takes with them. It could be a reminder, a collective call to action, a summary of your speech, or a story. For example: "It is upon us to choose the fate of our home, the earth by choosing to begin waste management at our personal spaces."

After concluding, add a few lines of gratitude to the audience for their time.

For example: "Thank you for being a wonderful audience and lending me your time. Hope this speech gave you something to take away."

Sample 1

Peer pressure is useful for the development of an individual. If there is no peer pressure at all then there would be no goal or aim to succeed. Write a speech on the topic -'Is Peer Pressure Beneficial or Not?' to be delivered on account of Children's Day celebration in your school. (150-200 words)

Answer: Respected Principal Sir, honourable teachers and my dear friends, on the occasion of Children's Day, I am going to present my views on the topic 'Is peer pressure beneficial or not?'

Peer pressure is beneficial as long as we know our limits. It is all upto us to be so strong, so firm, so unshakable and filled with conviction of not going on the wrong track.

Peer pressure is not always bad. Peers may teach you good habits and encourage you to follow them. Looking at what others do can help you bring a positive change in your way of thinking. Your peers, their choices and ways of life give you a glimpse of the world

outside the four walls of your house. What they think about things in life, how they perceive situations, how they react in different circumstances can actually expose you to the world around. Being part of a larger group of peers exposes you to the diversity in human behaviour. This makes you reflect on your behaviour and know where you stand. Peer pressure can lead you to make the right choices in life.

Your peers can, thus, influence the shaping of your personality in a positive way. Moreover, it's not pressure every time, sometimes it's inspiration, which makes you change for good.

Thank you.

Sample 2

Racism is bad. Anyone and everyone can be exposed to racism. Write a speech in 150-200 words on the topic 'Racism' to be delivered in the morning assembly of your school.

Answer: Respected Principal Sir, honourable teachers and my dear friends, good morning!

Why must I choose whom to befriend according to the colour of their skin? Is there anything written anywhere that makes one race above another? I am going to present my views on the topic 'Racism' today.

I am nobody to judge other people. In fact, we all are unique in our own way and we all should be judged on our individual and personal qualities.

We have lots of people who are filled with hatred-hatred pointed especially at the colour of the skin. But where does all this hatred come from? God has never conceived hate. Did he make us different just to see hatred and war? I don't think so. Why can't we carry out Martin Luther King's dream about a world in peace and without any kind of racism?

Racism works against the principle of being equal and the right of all people to be treated fairly. Hating people because of their colour or other factors is wrong. We all have to stay together and thus, we need to make the effort to embrace and accept other cultures. This can start with the simple act of friendship. Let us start today.

Thank you.

Sample 3

The actions and behaviour of senior college and university students are a far cry from the normal, decent and civilised. It's all the more reprehensible because even girls are subjected to indecency and vulgarity. Write a speech on the topic 'Ragging' in 150-200 words for your school's morning assembly.

Answer: Respected Principal Sir, honourable teachers and my dear friends, good morning!

Ragging deserves severe condemnation and needs to be consigned to the dustbin of discarded ideas. Today I am going to present my views on the serious issue of Ragging'

The practice has now become a source of uncivilised behaviour, which brings to the fore animal instincts of the practising youth. It deserves to be curtailed, curbed and ultimately abolished. It calls for strict action and punishment. Any mildness in this regard amounts to giving it a further fillip.

The raggers may put forth unsustainable arguments that it is meant to bring the freshers into the mainstream of campus life, that it helps in rounding up the angularities of the freshers who are awkward and uninitiated in the ways of college and university life. The supporters of ragging also hold forth that this results in understanding and mutual liking, which blooms into friendship. On the contrary, many ragging incidents result into attempted suicides. Youngsters are subjected to unwholesome and unhealthy practics. Such actions breed hostility and a strong desire to seek revenge. The ragged youngster nurses the humiliation in mind and next year, will take it out on a newcomer. The practice, thus, continues.

Hence, it calls for condemnation and a total ban of this practise of ragging, Thank you.

Sample 4

You are Ashok, studying in class XI-B. You have been asked by your Principal to speak in the morning assembly on 'The Importance of English'. Draft the speech in 150-200 words.

Answer: Good morning, respected Principal Sir, teachers and my friends. Today, I, Ashok of class XI-B, will highlight the importance of English in today's scenario.

English is a universal language which is now needed to be known by everyone. Without English, one feels handicapped. If you travel to any part of the world, and even to some parts of India, knowledge of English sees you through. That is why most public schools in cities are teaching in the English medium. The primary reason is that parents want their children to be fluent in English.

To get a reasonable job, it is a must to be able to write, understand and speak English, as it is the language of communication. Due to this, most of the interviews for good jobs and even admission interviews for colleges are conducted in English.

Many people wish to study or work abroad. To know the local language may be difficult and learning it would take time, but if one knows English, it comes to one's rescue. Even the best study materials for research work are available only in English. Computers which are widely used can usually be used only with knowledge of English.

Thus, English is a must in today's scenario. Thank you.

Debate Writing

A formal discussion on a particular technical or general topic during a public meeting or legislative gathering. In a debate, everyone puts their view and opinions in front of opposing ones and finally, one person wins the argument with a vote. But in debate writing, participating candidates need to express their views in a particular format and make opposing members impress by perfect debate writing skills.

Debate Writing

Want to flaunt your good English skills and abilities in an argument, discussion, or essay writing? Debate Writing is the best way to flaunt your hidden skills and gain confidence. Debates can be done verbally where a group of people put their views & opinions about the issue and expect you to deal with the raisen points or express your strong points against them.

Format of Debate Writing

In order to win any argument or discussion, one should gain more knowledge about the topic and then express their point of view in a perfect style of writing. So, here we have compiled a debate writing format to enhance your debate skills and make you win among all.

Formal Address

Formal addressing the chief guest, jury members and the audience is the great gesture of a debater. Hence, it is mandatory to address formally at the opening line of a debate.

Motion/Introduction: After addressing, the introduction about his/her is important to make their stand clear. The motion should be the first paragraph at the time of debate writing.

Argument/Discussion: Debater should put his/her views against other speakers and highlight the main lines by stressing or by giving real-time examples to make it more supportive. Your points must be strong and logical to revoke a few points stated by the opponent. The speaker should highlight all these main points of the debate or argument in the middle paragraph.

Conclusion: At the end of the debate lines also a speaker should express his/her own opinions regarding the issue. Basically, it needs to be an impactful statement that
everyone satisfies and stands on the issue. Make an end with gratitude like 'Thank You!'

Types of Debate

Students and participants can view several diverse formats or types of debates. Each and every debate type has its own unique style and focuses on the areas like school, college or a political arena. Following are some of the most general Debate Types that are pursued mostly in the western world. They are as follows:

- Parliamentary Debate
- Cross-Examination Debate
- Lincoln–Douglas Debate
- NDT Debate
- Spontaneous Argumentation
- Team Policy Debate

Easy Steps Writing a Debate Perfectly

Then, following these six easy steps help you give your best in framing good debate writing and make you win the verbal sparring match. Let's check the 6 simple steps below and write a debate with ease:

- Determining the Topic
- Economic Challenges
- Pre-research
- What's the Point?
- Use your own arguments
- Your Arguments
- Conclusion

Sample

You are chosen for representing your school at the regional level inter-school debate contest. Prepare a debate for the same on the topic given below: 'Newspapers ought to contain more news and fewer advertisements.

Answer: Respected Chairperson, August faculty and dear friends. I, Senha, stand before you to speak for the motion.

It is painful to see that journalists have lost all ethics and professionalism today. They adopt diverse techniques to increase the revenue of their paper. They try to sensationalise the news to win more readers. However, even the newspaper having the largest circulation is not self-dependent. It must have plenty of commercial advertisements to meet its running costs. In fact, it is these ads which provide the owners the requisite funds. Thus, advertisements cannot be ruled out. They are a necessary evil and must stay.

The owners and editors of the newspapers must also realise their responsibility to the nation. The press is the strongest pillar of democracy. It creates sensible public opinion in favour of good policies and criticises the wrong policies. The newspapers must maintain a balance between news and advertisements. A common man buys a newspaper for news. It would be better that the editors publish a classified advertisement supplement twice or thrice a week and save the general reader from the proliferation of advertisements while scanning the pages for views and news.
Academic excellence is the only requirement for a successful career." Write a debate either
for or against the motion. (120 – 150 words)

Academic Excellence Is the Only Requirement for A Successful Career

For The Motion
"The beautiful thing about learning is that no one can take it from you."
Respected judges and my worthy opponents, I stand before you all to speak in favour of the
motion: "Academic excellence is the only requirement for a successful career".

Right to Education is the fundamental right of every child in the age group of six to fourteen years. The education system in the primary years is designed so as to provide basic knowledge of each subject and help the youth of today to choose their subject of interest for its deeper study that can only be provided effectively through universities. It plays a key role in the development of society and nation. Information cannot be converted into knowledge without education. Education makes us capable of interpreting things, among other things.

It helps in raising future leaders by providing them clear understanding and developing decision making abilities. It makes them resourceful and competent. Excellence in academics prepares children for the competition ahead and teaches them to work hard as well.
Moreover, Excellency will ensure admission to the best universities for higher education that provide exposure and a kick start to their career. To conclude, I would say that one who has it's academic future choices sorted out, has it's career planned out.
"The goal of education is the advancement of knowledge and the dissemination of truth. "A
Thank you.

Against The Motion
Good morning, ladies and gentlemen! My topic for the day is "Academic excellence is the only requirement for a successful career" and I choose to speak against the motion.

"The goal of education is to raise the leaders of tomorrow". But my question is, how is it that most of the leaders of today happen to be college dropouts? This is because having degrees cannot ensure success. It fails to impart the life skills and polish personality of an individual. They can surely give you an overview of a subject but fail to provide an overview of how the world works. It does not ensure skills and competencies. It tells people what to think instead of how to think and the end results is that the society now has just robots who have switched their minds off only to believe what is being taught.

One's attitude towards life is what brings success. Undoubtedly, academic Excellencies can provide you degrees or may even land you at a job, but your success depends upon how you think, behave, walk, talk and present yourself. It has been rightly said, "Education produces great employees in the market, not employers".
Thank you.

Homes for the aged is a necessity in India '. Write a debate in 120- 150 words either for or against the motion. You are Shivam/ Shivani.

Homes For the Aged Is a Necessity in India

For The Motion
Old age is often referred to as the crown of life, as it is our play's last act. Honorable judges, teachers, and my worthy opponents, I thank you all for providing me the opportunity to highlight the importance of Old Age Homes in India.
An old age home is a place, a home for old people who have no one to look after them or those whose children have left them on the streets. The place, of course, is like a home where the inmates get all the facilities for a routine living, like food, clothing,

medicine and shelter. Old age brings with it physical weakness. In case they are alone at home while you're away, it would be almost impossible to tackle any medical emergency. These centers will take care of them and cater to all such emergencies Also, burglars usually attempt to break into a house where a lonely, aged person lives, murder them without hesitating and loot the house. That's why it is safer to keep your parents in a senior-care home when you have to stay away from them for your earning and are unable to keep them there with you.

Thus, it is crucial to have old age homes in the country because old age needs so little but needs that little very much. Nothing is more important than a smile that has struggled through tears and many years.
Thank you.

Against The Motion
Good morning, ladies, and gentlemen! My topic for the day is "Home for the aged is a
necessity in India "A and I choose to speak against the motion.

There is nothing fundamentally wrong with the whole idea of old age homes, but just like there are two sides of the same coin, it also has some disadvantages and problems associated to it. Services attract costs. Better the services, higher the costs. Most of the aged population are pensioners or dependent on children which makes it difficult for them to afford good quality care. There is a lack of privacy too. The environment is impersonal, which may give rise to feeling of loneliness, which may further lead to depression. They lose the right to decide what to eat and cannot spend time with grandchildren. Also, there have been many incidents of neglect and poor treatment.

They are those people who made us capable and created a world for us. How can we leave them in the cold, that too when they require the warmth of our love the most? Our parents have sacrificed so much for us without asking for anything in return. This makes it our sole responsibility to take care of them when they need it the most, because, in the end, the ultimate luxury is being at home and able to relax with the family.
Thank you.

Diary Writing

Maintaining a diary is generally a very good habit. Moreover, one can always check facts looking back, remember events, find an outlet and effectively document one's life this way. Also, some people even name their diaries and address them like an imaginary friend.

A personal journal is a private possession. In other words, this diary usually is just for you and it's not for public reading, so one can write liberally. But for the readers, diary entries are generally written differently.

How to Write a Diary

A Diary is a journal organized by date where you express your thoughts, feelings, opinions, and plans. So, be as candid as you can. Because this journal is your safe place. If you don't know where to start, then start by writing about your day, about yourself, and so on.

There are few points to keep in mind to write a diary

Always mention the date

Pick a corner and keep it for mentioning the dates of your diary entry. You may not write every day. Some people are also specific about time and place as well. Again, it's about personal preferences. Since one usually keeps a diary for a long period of time, it's wiser to think out a general format for your diary entries and stick to it. You may iterate and change a few things depending on how you feel like, no one's watching it. I personally choose the top left for mentioning the date.

Choose a subject

Just like a chapter, usually, there's a reason why you reached out to make a diary entry. For example, sometimes it's what happened that day or sometimes it is to write about something you want to do in the future or maybe to just mark an event that triggered a strong emotion in you like happiness, anger, excitement, etc. But whatever it is that you picked your journal for, your diary entry will have a topic that way.

Voice

Now, we always address our entries in the first person. If you want, you can give it a name. Usually, people address their diary entries as – "Dear Diary"

Be honest, it's you who are talking to

The key thing about a diary entry is that it is always kept truthful, natural and free-flowing. So, trust your thought train and don't stop or mince words for the fear of being watched or judged. As it is your space to let out all your feelings, so don't hold back. Make it a habit:

Well, this one, I personally think, you only have to remind yourself as you begin to write. Eventually, it sort of becomes this friend you reach out to automatically. Most of the times you will find it very therapeutic to maintain a diary. It's wonderful how when you let out all the emotions, sometimes the endings get quite conclusive and lead in a positive direction. Like you already knew the answer to your questions yourself. You just had to get all the foggy clouds of emotions out of your way to see it.

Sample

You went to receive your uncle and aunts from the Bangalore railway station. Write a diary where you share your experience of the journey from home to the railway station.

19th Jan 2021 Monday
9 PM
Dear Diary,

Today I went to Bangalore railway station, Yeshwantpura, to receive my uncle and aunt who were coming from Mumbai. It was a bright sunny day. Sun was shining like a star. While I and my father were crossing the Orion mall, we saw three elephants that made me reminded of my Kerala trip.

Last year I went on a Kerala trip, where we visited around 5 cities like Cochin, Wayanad, Munnar, Kovalam, and Alappuzha. All the places were really awesome and beautiful. Then we went to Elephant junction Thekkady, Kumily, where people go for elephant rides. I rode sitting above the elephant around for 2 and half hours. Then we have also done elephant bath and feeding. We took a lot of pictures with elephants. It was a nice trip and I still can't get over it.

Vikram
You recently visited the 24th Crafts Mela at Suraj Kund, Faridabad. It was Mini India assembled at one place. Using the hints, make a diary entry of what you saw and experienced there.

Hints
• More than 20 states of India represented
• Rajasthan—the theme state
• Participation of foreign countries
• cultural programmes, dances at 'Chaupal' and 'Rangmanch'
• Food courts catering all kinds of foods
• arts and handicrafts from the awarded artisans.

New Delhi
20th March, 20XX Monday, 8:00 pm

Dear Diary,
The Crafts Mela at Suraj Kund was much more impressive and grander than what I had imagined. This year the 'Theme State' was Rajasthan. The whole campus was painted with the visuals of Ranthambore, Chittor, Jodhpur and Jaisalmer. It was Mini India assembled on a few hundred acres of land. All the awarded artisans from different states had set up their workshops and stalls there. Many countries, more particularly Pakistan, Nepal and Afghanistan gave it an international look. Bangles, jewellery decoration pieces, wall-hangings, purses, shoes, sarees, garments and cosmetics found thousands of buyers. Every evening there were cultural shows at the 'Chaupal' and the 'Rangmanch'. The 'Food Court' provided all kinds of delicacies for food-lovers. Basically, it was India in all its colours, tastes and sounds scattered on the Aravalli hills.
Sameer

Informal letter

Introduction

Informal letters are personal letters that are written to let your friends or family know about what is going on in your life and to convey your regards. An informal letter is usually written to a family member, a close acquaintance or a friend. The language used in an informal letter is casual and personal.

Nowadays, it's quite rare to receive or write a letter to your friend. This is due to the use of instant messaging, emails and other technologies that make communication more immediate.

But, the excitement of receiving a letter remains. And, the act of writing a letter has its benefits too.
Setting time aside to write a letter to your friend, shows them you have been thinking of them and makes them feel special. Taking the time to write is also a great chance for you to express yourself and order your thoughts.

Types and Reasons to Write Informal Letters

You can literally write about anything you feel or think you want to convey. Informal letters can be written to inform your dear one about your success in a competition, about a movie you watched recently, about the trip that you would be going on, etc. It can also be to enquire about their well-being, to invite them to go along with you on a trip, to congratulate them on their new job, to convey your regards, etc. You can be as personal as you want when writing an informal letter.

Informal letters are written for a whole range of reasons you might write a letter to your friend to:

- Share news
- Say thank you
- Wish them a happy birthday
- Invite them to an event
- Congratulate them on something
- Apologise
- Tell them about a holiday

Features of an Informal Letters

Informal letters have different features in comparison to formal letters. They aren't as rigid in the way they are structured or written. And this means when you write a letter to your friend you can have some fun by breaking the usual letter writing rules. The way you structure your letter will depend on the type you are writing. But there are a few common features that are noticed when writing informally.
These are:

- A friendly opening and close
- A date
- Informal and chatty language
- Written in first person
- Paragraphs
- Addresses of the sender and recipient (depending on the type of letter)

Format and Key Points to Write an Informal Letter

Like any letter, there is a format to write an informal letter in English. Unlike a formal letter, an informal letter does not need to state something specific. It can be written in an easy, conversational style. They are in the nature of a friendly chat, so it can include a variety of topics. It can have all that you want to tell your dear one about. You can use colloquial expressions, unlike formal letters. There are a few easy guidelines that you can follow to be able to write impressive informal letters.

Address and Date: If you are thinking about how to start writing an informal letter, here is what you should know. To get your informal letter format right, you have to begin it with the sender's address. The address is written on the left-hand side of the paper. It is necessary that you write the complete address so that the receiver can write back to you. So, see to that you give the correct address along with the pin code. In case you are writing to someone in a different country, make sure you include your country in the address.
For example,
29, NBC Garden
Coimbatore – 641053

This is followed by the date. Writing the date is important as it would help the receiver know when exactly you had written the letter. You can write the date in either of the following formats:
For example,
15/11/2021 or 15th November 2021 or November 15, 2021

Forms of Greeting/Salutation: In informal letters to friends and family, you can address them by their names prefixed by qualifying terms such as Dear, My dear, Dearest, etc. You can also address them by their pet names (Eg: Dearest Rosy, Dear Andy, My dear Sweety...) or by their relationship with you (Dear Uncle, Dearest Grandma, My dear Cousin...). If you are writing to an ordinary friend who is older than you are, or of superior rank, it is respectful to use prefixes such as Mr, Mrs, Ms, etc. For example, Dear Mr Reddy.

Introduction and Body of the Letter: The words you use determine the nature of your letter. You can start your informal letter with an introduction to set the tone of the matter that is going to be discussed. You can begin by enquiring about the health and well-being of the recipient. For instance, I hope this letter of mine finds you in the pinkest of health. You can then explain the reason behind the letter and provide the details as elaborate as you wish to, unlike formal letters. The letter can be more like a friendly chat than an essay. You can write in a very casual and personal tone. If you are writing to an older person, do not use disrespectful terms or sentences.

Conclusion: End the informal letter on a friendly note. Use words in such a way that the recipient feels like they have had a wonderful time chatting with you. See to that you make sure you let them know that you would be awaiting their response to your letter.

Forms of Subscription/Signature: You can use the following in informal letters to relatives and near friends. Yours affectionately, Yours lovingly, Your loving friend, With love, etc., followed by your name (mostly your first name).
If you are writing to a close acquaintance whom you have addressed as Dear Mr, Mrs, etc., you can use Yours sincerely, Kind regards, etc.

Sample

Sample 1 - Letter to a friend about arranging a get-together BB Street,
Allahabad – 211005 12/02/2020

Dear Surya,
Hope you are keeping well, and everyone at home is keeping safe and healthy. It has been a long time since all of us have met, so I was thinking we could all meet up. I have planned to have a get-together next month. I would love to discuss more about it.
All of us could meet on Friday evening and stay over the weekend at a resort in Munnar. The climate in Munnar is great and it will be a good stress reliever. We could also go around the tourist spots if everyone is interested. If you are ready, we could talk to the others also. I will visit you next weekend to discuss more on this.
Awaiting your reply and hoping to meet you soon. Love,
Sreya

Sample 2 - Reply, regretting inability to join. 144, Stark Lane
Mumbai – 400054 15/02/2020

Dear Sreya,
It is extremely thoughtful of you to plan a get-together for all of us. I wish I could join you, but I am sorry to say that I have a project starting next month and it would not be possible for me to be there. If there is any way of preponing the get-together to any time before the month-end, I can definitely make it happen.
I hope we can reschedule the get-together and not miss the chance to meet up. Waiting to hear from you.
With love, Surya

Flamingo (Prose)

Chapter -1   The Last Lesson

Summary

Franz is Reluctant to go to School

Franz started for school very late that morning. His French teacher, M Hamel, had announced that he would question the class on participles. Poor Franz did not know even a single word about them and was afraid of a scolding from his teacher.

It was a bright sunny day and for a moment Franz thought of running away and spending the day outside. The chirping of birds and the marching of the Prussian soldiers was much more tempting than the rules of participles. However, Franz was able to fight the temptation and hurried off to school.

On his way to school, Franz passed the town hall and noticed a crowd in front of the bulletin board. For the past two years, all the bad news had come from it and Franz thought about what the matter was this time. As he was hurrying past, Wachter, the blacksmith, called out to him and said that there was plenty of time to reach the school. Franz thought that he was making fun of him and reached the school panting.

M Hamel's Strange Behavior

When Franz reached the school, he was very surprised to find that everything was quiet. Usually, when the school began, there would be a great commotion and activity. Franz had often counted on the commotion to get to his desk unnoticed. But, that day everything was as quiet as it was on a Sunday morning. Franz noticed that all of his classmates were already in their seats and M Hamel was walking up and down with his iron ruler under his arm.

He had to open the door and reach his seat in front of everybody. He was blushing and was very frightened. What surprised and confused him more was that, instead of scolding him, M Hamel spoke very kindly to him and told him to take his seat.

Franz Notices Many Unusual Things at School

After Franz had calmed down, he noticed that M Hamel was wearing a special attire, which he wore only on special occasions. The whole school was so strange and a seriousness prevailed in the atmosphere. But what surprised and confused him most was to see the village people sitting quietly on the back benches. They all looked very sad.

The Order from Berlin

Franz was still wondering as he observed the changes around him, when M Hamel mounted on his chair and made the dreadful announcement. He told the class that it was their last French lesson.

The order had come from Berlin to teach only German in the schools of Alsace and Lorraine and he would be leaving the school the next day. These words were a shock to little Franz. Now he remembered the gathering at the town hall. Franz was totally shocked by the sudden turn of events. He regretted not having learnt his lessons when there was still time.

Now, he will never be able to learn them. He had wasted his precious time away from the class, engaging himself in useless activities like seeking bird's eggs, going sliding on the Sarr river and so on. His books, which were a nuisance to him, suddenly felt like old friends. His feelings for his teacher too started changing.

The thought that M Hamel was going away and Franz would never see him again, made him forget all about how cranky M Hamel was. Franz was feeling very sorry for him. It was in honour of his 'last lesson' that he had put on his fine clothes, and the village people had gathered there to express their gratitude towards him, and to show their respect for their country and their language.

M Hamel Criticises Himself and the People of Alsace

While Franz was thinking of all this, he heard his name called out; it was his turn to recite. He would have given anything to be just able to say the rule loud and clearly. But unfortunately, he got mixed up on the first words. He was ashamed and stood holding his desk. M Hamel said that he would not scold him. He criticised the people of Alsace for their habit of putting off learning for some time in the future. He blamed their parents for not taking interest in their studies. He also blamed himself for this. Often, he sent the students to water his plants or gave them a holiday when he had wanted to go fishing.

Importance of Mother Tongue

M Hamel then talked about the French language. He called it the most beautiful, the clearest and the most logical language in the world. He wanted the people of France to reassure their language. According to him, whenever the people of a particular nation are enslaved, as long as they are an ached to their language, it is as if they have the key to their prison.

The Last Lesson

M Hamel opened a grammar book and taught them their last lesson. Franz was amazed to see how well he understood everything. Franz thought that probably he never paid much attention in the class and that M Hamel had never explained everything with so much patience. After that they had a lesson in writing.

M Hamel had brought new copies for them that day. Everyone was immersed in their work. Even the little children sitting in the class were tracing their fish hooks, as if that was French too.

The Final Good Bye

All this while, M Hamel sat motionless in his chair. Franz thought that M Hamel wanted to imprint this classroom scene in his mind. For 40 years, he had given his faithful service to the school and now his sister was packing their stuff. All this must have been really heart breaking for him. Finally, they had a lesson in history.

Everybody became emotional towards the end; some even started crying, but M Hamel had the courage and patience to hear every lesson to the last. Finally, as the church-clock struck twelve, M Hamel stood up. It was very evident that he had become emotional too. He tried to speak, but choked.

Question/Answer

Q1. What was Franz expected to be prepared with for school that day?
Ans: That day Franz was expected to be prepared with participles because M. Hamel had said that he would question them on participles. Franz did not know anything about participles.

Q2. What did Franz notice that was unusual about the school that day?
Ans: Usually, when school began, there was a great bustle, which could be heard out in the street. But it was all very still that day. Everything was as quiet as Sunday morning. There was no opening or closing of desks. His classmates were already in their places. The teacher's great ruler instead of rapping on the table, was under M. Hamel's arm.

Q3. What had been put up on the bulletin-board?
Ans: For the last two years all the bad news had come from the bulletin-board. An order had come from Berlin to teach only German in the schools of Alsace and Lorraine. The Germans had put up this notice on the bulletin-board.

Q4. What changes did the order from Berlin cause in school that day?
Ans: M. Hamel had put on his best dress—his beautiful green coat, his frilled shirt and the little black silk cap, all embroidered. The whole school seemed so strange and solemn. On the back benches that were always empty, the elderly village people were sitting quietly like the kids.

Q5. How did Franz's feelings about M. Hamel and school change?
Ans: Franz came to know that it was the last lesson in French that M. Hamel would give them. From the next day they will be taught only German. Then he felt sorry for not learning his lessons properly. His books, which seemed a nuisance and a burden earlier were now old friends. His feelings about M. Hamel also changed. He forgot all about his ruler and how cranky he was.

Chapter - 2   Lost Spring

Summary

Sometimes I Find a Rupee in the Garbage

Saheb: The Ragpicker

Every morning the author meets Saheb and his friends scrounging for 'gold' in the garbage dumps of her neighborhood. Saheb and his family hail from Bangladesh, but they have left their home a long time ago. Storms washed away their fields and homes, reducing them to a state of abject poverty, which they left behind in the hope of finding a better life. That is why they came to this city looking for 'gold'.

The author asks Saheb why he does rag picking and does not go to school. To this, he replies that there is no school in his neighborhood. The author jokingly promises to open a school. After a few days, Saheb asks if the author has opened the school. The author is very embarrassed at having made a promise that was not meant to be fulfilled.
Nevertheless, she realizes that such promises are made to these children almost every day.

Saheb-e-Alam: Lord of the Universe

After some months of knowing him, the author asks Saheb his full name. The author notices the irony in Saheb's name, 'Saheb-e-Alam,' which means Lord of the Universe. She feels that Saheb would not believe what his name means. Unaware of the meaning of his name, Saheb roams with his gang, barefoot, on the streets. The author curiously asks why they don't wear slippers. One replies that his mother does not bring them down from the shelf. Another says he wants shoes.
Moving across the country, the author has seen many children walking barefoot. One of the explanations is that it is a tradition and not lack of money. Anees wonders if this is just an excuse to explain away a perpetual state of poverty.

Author Pained by the Fact that Ragpickers are Still Barefoot

The author remembers a man from Udipi who, as a young boy, would pass a temple where his father was a priest and pray for a pair of shoes. Thirty years later the author visited his town. Behind the temple there was the house of a new priest. Anees noticed the young boy of the priest, who arrived panting. He was wearing shoes. The writer was reminded of the boy who prayed that he should never lose his shoes. The goddess had granted his prayer, as most of the young boys there now have shoes to wear. As against this, the ragpickers in the author's neighborhood still remain barefoot.

Garbage is Gold

The author's acquaintance with the barefoot ragpickers takes her to Seemapuri. Seemapuri is a place on the periphery of Delhi, yet miles away from it metaphorically. The place is home to 10000 other shoeless ragpickers like Saheb. They are all Bangladeshi refugees who came here back in 1971. They live in very poor conditions in mud structures with roofs of tin and tarpaulin.
The place has no running water facility and no drainage. The ragpickers have lived here for the past 30 years, some even more, without identity, yet they have valid ration cards. Not having an identity does not bother them, if at the end of the day they don't sleep with empty stomachs. They prefer to live here rather than in the fields at home which give them no grain.
They, who once lived in the beautiful land of green fields and rivers, are now compelled to pitch their tents wherever they find food.

Children are born in them and become partners in survival. And survival in Seema Puri means rag picking. Over the years, rag picking has become an art. Garbage is gold to these ragpickers. It is their only support and means of income. Saheb tells the author that sometimes he finds a rupee, even a ten-rupee note.
Aneesa realizes that garbage holds a different meaning to both parents and children. For parents it is the source of their livelihood, providing them with food and shelter; for children, it is wrapped in wonder.

Lost Spring

One winter morning, the author sees Saheb outside the fenced gate of the neighborhood club. He is watching a game of tennis. Saheb seems to be fascinated by the game. He tells the author that sometimes the guard lets him in and then he can ride the swing. The author notices that Saheb is wearing tennis shoes. Saheb tells her that someone gave them to him. The fact that some rich boy discarded the shoes because there was a hole in one of them does not bother him. For Saheb, who has walked his whole life barefoot, it is like a dream come true.

Saheb No Longer his Own Master

One morning the author sees Saheb on his way to the milk booth. He is carrying a steel canister. He informs the author that now he works at the tea stall and is paid ₹ 800 and all his meals.

But the author feels that Saheb is not happy. His face has lost its carefree look. The steel canister seems heavier than the plastic bag. The bag was his, but the canister belongs to the owner of the tea stall. Saheb is no longer his own master.

I Want to Drive a Car

Mukesh Wants to be his Own Master

Here begins the second story. In Firozabad, the author meets Mukesh, who insists on being his own master. He wishes to be a motor mechanic. Anees asks him if he knows anything about cars. Mukesh replies that he wants to learn to drive a car.

The author feels that his dream is like a mirage amidst the dusty streets of Firozabad. Every second family in Firozabad is engaged in the business of bangle-making. Firozabad is the center of India's glass-blowing industry, where generations after generations have been involved in this business.

Another Encounter with Poverty

The people of Firozabad involve their children in the bangle-making industry without knowing that it is illegal for children to work in the glass furnaces with high temperatures, in dingy cells without air and light. If the -law is enforced, almost 20000 children would be out of the hot furnaces, where they work day and night, often losing the brightness of their eyes.
Mukesh proudly announces that his house is being rebuilt, and volunteers to take the author home. They walk down stinking lanes choked with garbage, past houses that are small and dirty constructions with wobbly doors and with no windows, where families of humans and animals co-exist in a primitive state.

They enter a half-built shack, one part of which is thatched with dead grass, where a frail young woman is cooking the evening meal for the whole family. She is the wife of Mukesh's elder brother. Though not much older in years, she has the respect of a bahu. She veils her face when Mukesh's father enters.

The God-given Lineage

Mukesh's father has toiled hard all his life, first as a tailor and then as a bangle-maker. Still the poor fellow has been unable to renovate his house or send his two sons to school.

All he could manage to do was to teach them what he knows about the art of bangle-making. Mukesh's grandmother has seen her husband go blind with the dust from polishing the glass bangles. She believes in destiny. "Can a God-given lineage ever be broken?" she implies. Born in the caste of bangle-makers, they have seen nothing but bangles-bangles of various colours.

Lost Spring

In dark hutments, next to lines of flames of flickering oil lamps, sit boys and girls with their fathers and mothers, welding pieces of coloured glass into circles of bangles. Their eyes are more adjusted to the dark than to the light outside. They often end up losing their eyesight before they become adults. The author notices a young girl, Savita, in a drab pink dress, sitting beside an elderly woman, helping in making bangles. Her hands move like a machine.

Anees wonders if she understands the sanctity of the bangles for Indian women. The sad irony will suddenly dawn upon her. She will become a bride like the old woman sitting beside her. In a voice drained of joy, the old lady tells the author that she has not enjoyed even one full meal in her entire lifetime.

Daring, Not a Part of Growing Up

One wonders if Mukesh's father has achieved what many have failed to achieve in their lifetime. He has a roof over his head. The cry of not having money can be heard in every household of Firozabad. Nothing has changed over the years. Years of hardship have killed all hopes and dreams.

The author asks a group of young men to organize themselves in a cooperative. She learns the horrific truth that even if they get organized, they are taken to jail for doing something illegal and are beaten up. There is no leader among them.
The author finds two distinct worlds in Firozabad. One is the exploited family caught in a vortex of poverty and the stigma of the caste in which they were born. The other is a vicious circle of those who exploit them, the shikars, the middlemen, the politicians, the lawmakers, the policemen and the bureaucrats. These have created such a burden that a child accepts this as naturally as its father did. To do something else would mean to dare. And daring is not a part of growing up.

A Ray of Hope

The author is filled with joy when she finds that Mukesh thinks differently. The boy is filled with hope. His dream of being a motor-mechanic is still alive in his eyes.

He is willing to dare. Anees asks Mukesh if he also dreams of flying a plane. Mukesh replies in the negative. He is content to dream of cars, as few planes fly over Firozabad.

Question/Answer

Q1. What is Saheb looking for in the garbage dumps? Where is he and where has he come from?
Ans: Saheb is looking for gold in the garbage dumps. He is in the neighborhood of the author. Saheb has come from Bangladesh. He Came with his mother in 1971. His house was set amidst the green fields of Dhaka. Storms swept away their fields and homes. So they left the country.

Q2. What explanations does the author offer for the children not wearing footwear?
Ans: One explanation offered by the author is that it is a tradition to stay barefoot. It is not lack of money. He wonders if this is only an excuse to explain away a perpetual state of poverty. He also remembers the story of a poor body who prayed to the goddess for a pair of shoes.

Q3. Is Saheb happy working at the tea-stall? Explain.
Ans. No, Saheb is not happy working at the tea-stall. He is no longer his own master. His face has lost the carefree look. The steel canister seems heavier than the plastic bag he would carry so lightly over his shoulder. The bag was his. The canister belongs to the man who owns the tea-shop.

Q4. What makes the city of Firozabad famous?
Ans: The city of Firozabad is famous for its bangles. Every other family in Firozabad is engaged in making bangles. It is the center of India's glass-blowing industry. Families have spent generations working around furnaces, welding glass, making bangles for the women in the land.

Q5. Mention the hazards of working in the glass bangles industry?
Ans: Boys and girls with their fathers and mothers sit in dark hutments, next to lines of flames of flickering oil lamps. They weld pieces of coloured glass into circles of bangles. Their eyes are more adjusted to the dark than to the light outside. They often end up losing eyesight before they become adults. Even the dust from polishing the glass of bangles is injurious to eyes. Many workers have become blind. The furnaces have very high temperature and therefore very dangerous.

Chapter - 3   Deep Water

Summary

The Narrator Developed an Aversion to Water at a Young Age

The narrator recalls a horrific incident that happened to him when he was ten or eleven years old. He had decided to learn swimming, and the YMCA pool gave him the opportunity, as it was safe. It was only two or three feet deep at the shallow end and, while it was nine feet deep at the other end, the drop was gradual. In comparison, the Yakima river was treacherous. The narrator's mother continually warned him against it. She kept reminding him about the details of each drowning incident in the river. The narrator developed an aversion to water at the age of three or four when his father took him to the beach in California. The waves knocked him down and swept over him. He was buried in water and was breathless. He was terrorized by the strong force of the waves, but his father had only laughed.

The Misadventure

The introduction to the pool revived the narrator's unpleasant memories and stirred his childhood fears. Still, he tried to learn swimming by imitating the other boys. He was just beginning to feel at ease in the water when a mishap occurred. He went to the pool one day and found that no one else was there. He was timid about going in alone. So, he sat on the side of the pool to wait for others. Just then a big bully came. He was quite muscular. He picked up Douglas and threw him into the deep end of the pool. Douglas landed in a sitting position, swallowed water, and went at once to the bottom.

Douglas Tried to Save His life

The narrator was frightened, but not frightened out of his mind. He made a plan to save himself. When his feet would hit the bottom, he would make a big jump, come to the surface, lie flat on it and paddle to the edge of the pool. However, the nine feet down seemed more like ninety to poor Douglas.

He was totally out of breath when his feet touched the bottom. Still, with all his strength, he made a spring upwards. He came up slower than he had thought. He opened his eyes and saw nothing but water. He started to panic. Douglas was suffocating and tried to yell but no sound came out.

A Sheer, Stark Terror

Then he came up to the surface and started beating the surface of the water. He tried to breathe, but swallowed water and choked. Douglas tried to bring his legs up, but they hung like dead weights. A great force was taking him to the bottom of the pool.

He had lost all his breath. His lungs ached and his head throbbed. But he remembered his strategy. He opened his eyes and saw nothing but water with a yellow glow. A sheer, stark terror seized him. terror that knew no understanding, terror that knew no control, a terror that only the one who had experienced it could understand. He was shrieking under water.

Only his heart and the pounding in his head said that he was still alive. Douglas told himself that he had to remember to jump when he reached the bottom. He again jumped with all his might, but his jump went in vain. He was still under water. The stark terror took him more tightly in its clutches.

The Fight for Survival is Lost

Douglas describes how fear paralyzed him. His arms and legs stopped moving. He trembled with fright. He tried to call for his mother, but nothing happened. Suddenly, Douglas found himself coming out of the water. He sucked for air and got water. Then he started going down for the third time. Then all his efforts ceased and his body went limp. A blackness took over his brain which wiped out fear and terror. Everything went quiet and peaceful. Douglas felt as if he was wrapped in his mother's arms. Then he fell unconscious. The next thing he remembers was lying on his stomach beside the pool, vomiting.

The Terror Destroyed Douglas' Social Life, He Tried to Overcome it

Douglas couldn't eat that night. He was weak and trembling. He shook and cried on his bed. He never went back to the pool. He feared water and avoided it whenever he could. Whenever he went near water, the terror that had seized him in the pool would return to haunt him. The fear paralyzed him.

This handicap stayed with him as years rolled by. It ruined his fishing trips and deprived him of the joy of canoeing, boating and swimming. He tried his best to overcome this fear, but it didn't let go of him. Finally, Douglas decided to get a swimming instructor. He went to a pool and practiced five days a week, an hour each day. The instructor put a belt with a rope around Douglas.

This rope went through a pulley. The instructor held on to the other end of the rope. Each time the instructor relaxed his hold on the rope and Douglas went under, some of the old terror returned and froze his legs. It took him three months to get over this fear.

Then the instructor taught him to breathe while swimming. Next he taught him to move his legs. Thus, piece by piece, bit by bit, he built a swimmer out of Douglas.

Douglas' Will to Live Grew in Intensity

After the training was finished, Douglas wondered if he would be terror-stricken when he would be alone in the pool. He tried, and tiny vestiges of the old terror did return, but now he was not afraid. Douglas was still not satisfied. So, he went to Lake Wentworth in New Hampshire and swam two miles across the lake. When Douglas was in the middle of the lake, he put his face under and saw nothing but bottomless water.

The old sensation came back to haunt him. But this time Douglas was strong. He swam on. Yet he had some residual doubts. At his first opportunity, he went to the Warm Lake. He swam to the other shore and back. He was thrilled with joy, as he had conquered his fear of water. The experience had a deep meaning for him.

He explains that death was peaceful but it was the fear of death that crippled a person. Here he quotes President Roosevelt, saying, 'All we have to fear is fear itself.' Because he had experienced death and the terror that it could produce, his will to live somehow grew in intensity.

Question/Answer

Q1. What is the "misadventure " that William Douglas speaks about?

Ans: William O. Douglas had just learnt swimming. One day, an eighteen-year-old big bruiser picked him up and tossed him into the nine feet deep end of the Y.M.C.A. pool. He hit the water surface in a sitting position. He swallowed water and went at once to the bottom. He nearly died in this misadventure.

Q2. What were the series of emotions and fears that Douglas experienced when he was thrown into the pool? What plans did he make to come to the surface?

Ans: Douglas was frightened when he was thrown into the pool. However, he was not frightened out of his wits. While sinking down he made a plan. He would make a big jump when his feet hit the bottom. He would come to the surface like a cork, lie flat on it, and paddle to the edge of the pool.

Q3. How did this experience affect him?

Ans: This experience revived his aversion to water. He shook and cried when he lay on his bed. He couldn't eat that night. For many days, there was a haunting fear in his heart. The slightest exertion upset him, making him wobbly in the knees and sick to his stomach. He never went back to the pool. He feared water and avoided it whenever he could.

Q4. Why was Douglas determined to get over his fear of water?

Ans: His fear of water ruined his fishing trips. It deprived him of the joy of canoeing, boating, and swimming. Douglas used every way he knew to overcome this fear he had developed 'since childhood. Even as an adult, it held him firmly in its grip. He determined to get an instructor and learn swimming to get over this fear of water.

Q5. How did the instructor "build a swimmer" out of Douglas?

Ans: The instructor built a swimmer out of Douglas piece by piece. For three months he held him high on a rope attached to his belt. He went back and forth across the pool. Panic seized the author every time. The instructor taught Douglas to put his face under water and exhale and to raise his nose and inhale. Then Douglas had to kick with his legs for many weeks till these relaxed. After seven months the instructor told him to swim the length of the pool.

Chapter - 4   The Rattrap

Summary

The Rattrap Peddler and his Thoughts About the World

Once upon a time, there was a vagabond who went around selling small rattraps. He made them from the material he got by begging. The business was not profitable, so he had to beg and even steal to survive. His clothes were in rags, his cheeks were sunken and hunger gleamed in his eyes.

While he was engrossed in his thoughts about rattraps one day, a very amusing thought came to his mind that the world was a big rattrap. It offered comforts and joys just like the rattrap offered cheese and pork. As soon as a rat was tempted to touch the bait, it trapped him.

The Crofter Treats the Peddler Nicely but the Peddler Cheats him

One dark evening, as the peddler was trudging along the road, he went to a small grey cottage, seeking shelter for the night. The owner, who had once been a crofter, not only invited him in, but was happy to get someone to talk to. The crofter, who had no wife or children, was very talkative and shared much about himself with the peddler. He informed the peddler that during his days of prosperity, he worked at the Ramsjö Ironworks. Now, his cow supported him. He even shared the fact that he had earned thirty kronor by selling the cow's milk. The guest seemed incredulous, so the crofter showed him the money, also revealing where it was kept. Next day, both left the cottage at the same time. But, half an hour later the peddler returned. He went up to the window, smashed a pane and took out the thirty kronor from the pouch in which they were kept.

The Vagabond is Pleased with his Smartness; Gets Lost in the Woods

The vagabond was quite pleased with his smartness. He avoided the public highway and turned into the wood, as he felt he would be safer and no one would be able to catch him. It was a big and confusing forest. He tried to walk in a definite direction, but the paths twisted back and forth so strangely that he was confused. He walked on and on and soon realised that he had been walking around in the same part of the forest.

All at once, he recalled his thoughts about the world being a rattrap. Now, his own turn had come. He had let himself be fooled by the bait and had been caught in a rattrap. The entire forest, with its trees, trunks and branches, seemed to him like a prison that offered no escape.

The Peddler Meets the Ironmaster; Declines his Invitation

Finally, the peddler saw no way out. He was so overwhelmed with exhaustion that he sank down to the ground, tired to death, thinking that his last moment had come. Just then, he heard the sound of the regular thumping of a hammer. He realised that the sound was coming from an iron mill. He summoned all his strength and walked in the direction of the sound.

He reached the Ramsjö Ironworks, which was then a large plant with smelter, rolling mill and forge. He entered the ironworks amidst the different sounds coming from the work going on in full swing. It was quite usual for persons like him to be attracted by the warmth and shelter of the forge, so he was ignored by the blacksmiths. The master blacksmith rather haughtily granted him permission to stay.

Soon, the ironmaster came into the forge for his inspection and noticed the peddler. He mistook him in the dim light for an old regimental comrade and addressed him as Nils Olof. The peddler didn't try to clear his doubt, as he thought the ironmaster might give him some money. The ironmaster invited him home. The peddler thought that going to the manor house would be like 'throwing himself voluntarily into the lion's den'. So, he declined the invitation.

Ironmaster Sends his Daughter Edla to Persuade the Peddler

The ironmaster assumed that the Peddler felt embarrassed because of his miserable clothing. He tried to comfort the peddler by informing him that there was nothing to be ashamed about. He further told him that his wife Elizabeth was dead, his sons were settled abroad and he lived with his daughter Edla. But the tramp constantly refused to go with him. The ironmaster went away, but he was not deterred by the peddler's persistent refusal. He sent his daughter to persuade the peddler. When Edla came to the ironworks, she found the man alarmed and frightened.

She tried to comfort him. She somehow sensed that his fear conveyed that he was either a thief on the run or an escaped prisoner. Still, she was very friendly and kind to the peddler. The peddler felt confidence in her and accepted the invitation. He felt guilty and cursed himself for stealing the crofter's money.

Edla Expresses her Doubts About the Peddler

The next day was Christmas Eve. The ironmaster was happy that he would be spending his time with an old friend. He told Edla that they needed to feed him well and provide him with a better business than selling rattraps. Edla said that she was doubtful about the peddler, as he didn't display the slightest sign of being educated. However, the ironmaster told her to have some patience. Just then the door opened and the stranger entered the room. He was now well groomed. He was wearing clothes which belonged to the ironmaster.

The Ironmaster Gets Angry; the Peddler Retaliates

The ironmaster realized that the tramp was no friend of his. The peddler made no attempt to delude them any longer. He explained that he never said to the ironmaster that he was Nils Olof. He had even pleaded and begged for not coming to the manor house. He added that no harm had been done and he could put on his rags and go away. The ironmaster said that the peddler had not been very honest and he would take him to the Sheriff. The peddler got agitated. He said that the world was like a big rattrap, and some day the ironmaster would also be tempted to touch the bait and would be doomed. The ironmaster started laughing.

Edla Argues on Behalf of the Peddler

The ironmaster asked the peddler to leave. But Edla wanted him to stay back. She felt that they had promised the peddler Christmas cheer, and it would be wrong to send him away. The peddler was surprised by this gesture. Edla further added that the peddler must have been through a bad time, as he was always chased away. He could not even sleep unafraid.

The ironmaster gave in. The peddler was allowed to stay on for Christmas, but the only thing he did was to sleep soundly after that. Once or twice he was woken up to have food but besides that, he only slept. It seemed as though he had never slept as quietly and safely. The ironmaster and Edla gifted him the suit that he was wearing as a Christmas present. She told him that he was welcome to spend even the next Christmas with them. The peddler kept staring at her in boundless amazement.

The Peddler Becomes a Changed Man

The next morning the ironmaster and his daughter went to the church for Christmas service, leaving the peddler at home. They returned home and Edla was very sad. At the church, they had learned that a rattrap peddler robbed an old crofter who once worked at their Ramsjö Ironworks. The ironmaster was furious.

They thought that by the time they would reach home, the peddler would have escaped with all their silver and other valuables. When they got home, the ironmaster asked the valet if the peddler was still there. The valet informed him that the fellow had left but he had not taken anything with him. Instead, he had left something for Edla. Edla opened the package and found a rattrap. In the rattrap were three wrinkled ten kronor notes and a letter.

The peddler had written that since Edla had treated him like a real captain, he also wanted to be nice to her. He wanted the money to be returned to the crofter. He further wrote that he would not have been able to escape the rattrap, if he had not been raised to the status of a captain. He even signed the letter as 'Captain von Stahle'. He was a changed man.

Question/Answer

Q1. From where did the peddler get the idea of the world being a rattrap?
Ans: The peddler had been thinking of his rattraps when suddenly he was struck by the idea that the whole world was nothing but a big rattrap. It existed only to set baits for people. It offered riches and joys, shelter and food, heat and clothing in the same manner as the rattrap offered cheese and pork. As soon as someone let himself be tempted to touch the bait, it closed in on him, and then everything came to an end.

Q2. Why was he amused by this idea?
Ans: His own life was sad and monotonous. He walked laboriously from place to place. The world had never been kind to him. So, during his gloomy ploddings, this idea became his favourite pastime. He was amused how people let themselves be caught in the dangerous snare and how others were still circling around the bait.

Q3. Did the peddler expect the kind of hospitality that he received from the crofter?
Ans: The crofter served him porridge for supper and tobacco for his pipe. He also played a game of cards with him till bed time. This hospitality was unexpected as people usually made sour faces when the peddler asked for shelter.

Q4. Why was the crofter so talkative and friendly with the peddler?
Ans: The crofter's circumstances and temperament made him so talkative and friendly with the peddler. Since he had no wife or child, he was happy to get someone to talk to in his loneliness. Secondly, he was quite generous with his confidences.

Q5. Did the peddler respect the confidence reposed in him by the crofter?
Ans: No, the peddler did not respect the confidence reposed in him by the crofter. At the very first opportunity that he got, he smashed the window pane, took out the money and hung the leather pouch back in its place. Then he went away.

Chapter - 5   Indigo

Summary

Rajkumar Shukla 'The Resolute Peasant'

Gandhi starts narrating the incident which made him decide to spur the exit of the British from India. The incident occurred in 1917. Gandhi had gone to the December 1916 annual convention of the Indian National Congress Party in Lucknow. A poor and emaciated peasant, Rajkumar Shukla, approached Gandhi there. Shukla was one of the sharecroppers of Champaran. Shukla wanted Gandhi to visit his district and look into the condition of the peasants there. He came to the Congress Session to complain about the injustice of the landlord system in Bihar.

Gandhi had other commitments but Shukla accompanied him everywhere for weeks, he never left Gandhi's side. Gandhi was very impressed by his tenacity and agreed to accompany him to Champa ran. He told him to come to Calcutta and take him from there. When Gandhi went to Calcutta after some months, he found Shukla already present there.

Visit to Rajendra Prasad's House and then to Muzaffarpur

Shukla and Gandhi went to Patna, Bihar, to meet a lawyer named Rajendra Prasad, the man who later became the President of the Congress Party and of India. Rajendra Prasad was out of town. The servants knew Shukla as a poor peasant who pestered their master to help the indigo sharecroppers. As Gandhi accompanied him, they thought him to be another farmer. Gandhi was not allowed to drink water from the well as they thought he was an untouchable.

Gandhi decided to visit Muzaffarpur before Champaran to obtain more complete information about the conditions prevalent in the area.
Gandhi sent a telegram to Professor JB Kriplani, who received them at the station with a large body of students. Gandhi stayed in Muzaffarpur for two days in the home of Professor Malkani, a government school teacher.
He recalled that his stay in the house of a government servant was an extraordinary thing in those days'. In smaller localities, the Indians were afraid to show sympathy for advocates of home rule.

Gandhi Scolded the Lawyers

The news of Gandhi's arrival spread like wildfire. Sharecroppers from Champaran began arriving in large numbers. Muzaffarpur lawyers met Gandhi. They told him about their cases and reported the size of their fee.

Gandhi scolded the lawyers for collecting a huge fee from the poor sharecroppers. Gandhi concluded that the peasants were so crushed and fear-stricken that going to law courts was useless. The real relief for them was to be free from fear.
The Sharecropping Arrangement

Most of the land fit for cultivation in Champaran was divided into large estates owned by Englishmen. They forced the Indian tenants to plant 15% of their holdings with indigo and surrender the entire indigo harvest as rent.
After the landlords learned that Germany had developed synthetic indigo, they asked for compensation from the sharecroppers for being released from the 15% arrangement. The sharecropping arrangement was irksome and so many peasants signed willingly.

However, some of them engaged lawyers. Meanwhile, the news of synthetic indigo reached the sharecroppers and they felt cheated, unhappy and then became resentful. They wanted their money back.
Gandhi Disobeys the Official Order

It was amidst such chaos that Gandhi arrived in Champaran. He visited the Secretary of the British landlord's association in order to piece together all the facts. He was met with resistance. The Secretary told him that no information would be given to an outsider. Gandhi answered that he was no outsider. He then visited the British Commissioner. Gandhi reported that he was bullied and asked to leave Tirhut. Gandhi proceeded to Motihari, the capital of it Champaran. A vast multitude greeted him. Using a house as headquarters, he continued his investigations. A report came that a peasant had been maltreated in a nearby village. Gandhi decided to check the matter himself.

On the way, he was ordered by a police superintendent's messenger to return to the town. Thereafter, he was served with an official notice to quit Champaran. Gandhi signed a receipt of the notice and further wrote that he would disobey the order. As a result, he was summoned to appear in the court the next day.
Spontaneous Demonstration of the Peasants

Gandhi could not sleep the whole night. He telegraphed Rajendra Prasad to come from Patna with influential friends and sent instructions to the ashram. He also wired a full report to the Viceroy.

Next day, several thousand peasants reached Motihari and started demonstrating around the courthouse. They had merely heard that a certain Mahatma who wanted to help them was in trouble with the authorities. Gandhi felt that this was the beginning of their liberation from fear of the British The officials felt powerless, but Gandhi helped them regulate the crowd. He gave them proof that the British tyranny will no longer be borne. The government was baffled.

The trial was postponed. Gandhi protested against the delay. He confessed that he broke the law but only because of the voice of his conscience. The magistrate announced a two hour recess and asked Gandhi to get a bail prepared. Gandhi refused. The judge didn't deliver the judgement for days and Gandhi was allowed to remain at liberty.

Gandhi Influences the Lawyers

Rajendra Prasad, along with many prominent lawyers, conferred with Gandhi. Gandhi asked them what they would do if he was sent to jail. The senior lawyer replied that they were there to help Gandhi; if he was arrested, they would go home. Gandhi reprimanded them about the injustice to the sharecroppers.

The lawyers consulted among themselves. They thought that when Gandhi, a total stranger, was ready to go to jail for the sake of the peasants in their region, it would be shameful for them if they left the peasants, whom these lawyers claimed to serve. They told Gandhi that they were ready to follow him to jail. Gandhi exclaimed, 'The battle of Champaran is won'.

Civil Disobedience Triumphs, Lieutenant-Governor Summons Gandhi

Gandhi was informed that the Lieutenant-Governor of the province had ordered the case to be dropped. Civil disobedience had triumphed for the first time in modern India.
Inquiries into the grievances of the farmers over a wide area began. About ten thousand testimonials were reported. Notes were made of the evidence. The whole area throbbed with activity and the landlords protested vehemently against the inquiries.
In June, the Lieutenant-Governor, Sir Edward Gait, summoned Gandhi. Gandhi laid out detailed plans for civil disobedience if he did not return from the summons. The Lieutenant-Governor, after having four protracted meetings with Gandhi, appointed an official commission to enquire into the situation. Gandhi was the sole representative of the peasants in the commission.

Gandhi Agrees to 25% Compensation

The evidence against the landlords was overwhelming. They asked Gandhi how much they should repay. They thought he would demand full repayment of the money which was illegally and deceitfully extorted from the sharecroppers. Gandhi asked for only 50%. The landlords offered to refund 25%. To everybody's surprise, Gandhi agreed.

Gandhi explained that the amount of the refund was not important. What mattered was that the landlords were obliged to surrender part of the money, and with it, part of their prestige. The planters behaved as lords above the law, but after this incident, the peasants saw that they had rights and persons to defend them. They learned courage.

The Poor Conditions of Champaran and Gandhi's Typical Methods

Gandhi wanted to do something about the cultural and social backwardness in the Champaran villages immediately. He called for volunteers to help. His wife Kasturba and his youngest son also arrived to help. Primary schools were opened in six villages. Kasturba taught the ashram rules on personal cleanliness and community sanitation. Castor oil, quinine and sulphur ointment were given to the ailing.

Gandhi noticed the filthy state of women's clothes. He asked Kasturba to talk to them about it. One woman took Kasturba into her hut. She showed her that there were no boxes or cupboards for clothes. The sari that she was wearing was the only one she had. Gandhi kept a long distance watch on the ashram. He sent regular instructions by post and asked for financial accounts. The Champaran episode was a turning point in Gandhi's life. He explained that what he did was an ordinary thing. He declared that the British could not order him about in his own country.

Champaran was an attempt to free the poor peasants from exploitation and it didn't begin as an act of defiance. This was the typical Gandhi pattern. His politics were intertwined with the practical day-to-day problems of the millions.

Self-reliance-The Making of a Free Indian

In all the things that Gandhi did, he tried to mold a new free Indian, who could stand on his own feet and thus make India free. Charles Freer Andrews, an English pacifist, who had become a devoted follower of Gandhi, came to bid him goodbye. Gandhi's lawyer friends wanted Andrews to help them. Gandhi strongly opposed the suggestion.

According to him, asking for Andrews' help was showing the weakness of their hearts. He assured them the cause was just and they must rely upon themselves to win the battle.

Gandhi in this way taught them a lesson on self-reliance. Self-reliance, Indian independence and help to the sharecroppers were all bound together.

Question/Answer

Q1. Why is Rajkumar Shukla described as being 'resolute'?

Ans: He had come all the way from Champaran district in the foothills of Himalayas to Lucknow to speak to Gandhi. Shukla accompanied Gandhi everywhere. Shukla followed him to the ashram near Ahmedabad. For weeks he never left Gandhi's side till Gandhi asked him to meet at Calcutta.

Q2. Why do you think the servants thought Gandhi to be another peasant?

Ans: Shukla led Gandhi to Rajendra Prasad's house. The servants knew Shukla as a poor yeoman. Gandhi was also clad in a simple dhoti. He was the companion of a peasant. Hence, the servants thought Gandhi to be another peasant.

Q3. List the places that Gandhi visited between his first meeting with Shukla and his arrival at Champaran.

Ans: Gandhi's first meeting with Shukla was at Lucknow. Then he went to Cawnpore and other parts of India. He returned to his ashram near Ahmedabad. Later he went to Calcutta, Patna and Muzaffarpur before arriving at Champaran.

Q4. What did the peasants pay the British landlords as rent? What did the British now want instead and why? What would be the impact of synthetic indigo on the prices of natural indigo?

Ans: The peasants paid the British landlords indigo as rent. Now Germany had developed synthetic indigo. So, the British landlords wanted money as compensation for being released from the 15 per cent arrangement. The prices of natural indigo would go down due to the synthetic Indigo.

Q5. The events in this part of the text illustrate Gandhi's method of working. Can you identify some instances of this method and link them to his ideas of Satyagraha and non-violence?

Ans: Gandhi's politics was intermingled with the day-to-day problems of the millions of Indians. He opposed unjust laws. He was ready to court arrest for breaking such laws and going to jail. The famous Dandi March to break the 'salt law' is another instance. The resistance and disobedience was peaceful and a fight for truth and justice…This was linked directly to his ideas of Satyagraha and non-violence.

Summary

The Make-up Department of Gemini Studios

The make-up department was in a building which was said to be Robert Clive's erstwhile stable. In the studios, the make-up material with the brand name 'Pancake' was used profusely. All actresses of yesteryears were familiar with it. The author feels that modern actresses may not be aware of its existence.

The author mocks Robert Clive by saying that during his short life he is said to have lived in a number of residences in Madras. He fought battles and even got married here.

A Vivid Description of the Make-up room

The make-up room looked like a hair-cutting salon. It was crowded with large mirrors and flooded with light. It was not a very pleasing experience to get the make-up done because of the heat from the dazzling lights.

The Make-up Department and National Integration

The department was initially headed by a Bengali. He was succeeded by a Maharashtrian who was assisted by a Dharwar Kannadiga. Then different people belonging to different states occupied the position there. The author points out that all this shows that the make-up department was an ideal specimen of national integration. The author jokingly tells the readers about the 'skills' of these make-up men. With quite a lot of Pancake and other potions and lotions, they could mar the beauty of any person. However, Asokamitran clarifies by saying that perhaps the hideous crimson coloured make-up was important to look presentable on the screen.

A Strict Hierarchy in the Make-up Department

An elaborate division of work marked the make-up department. The chief make-up man dressed up the actors in lead roles. His senior assistant looked after the 'second' hero and heroine while the junior assistant took charge of the main comedian. The players who played the crowd were looked after by the office boy of the department.

The Office Boy

The office boy was not exactly a boy. He was in his early forties. He joined the studio years back and aspired to be a top film star or top screen writer, director or lyric writer. He also wrote poetry. On the days of crowd-shooting, he mixed the make-up material on a large scale and painted faces.

The Narrator's Work in the Studio

The narrator worked in a cubicle. His work was to cut newspaper clippings and store them in files. Everybody thought that his work was next to nothing and so he was continuously lectured by other employees. The office boy often came to his cubicle and gave vent to his feelings of frustration and irritation. The narrator desperately wished to escape from his continuous tirade and prayed for crowd shooting.

Kothamanglam Subbu

He was the No. 2 at Gemini Studios. According to the office boy, Subbu did not deserve anything because he was neither well educated nor had any exceptional talent. His only virtue was being a Brahmin, due to which he got opportunities readily. He was always cheerful. Even a flop film in which he had a hand couldn't take away his cheerfulness. The narrator takes a dig at him by saying that he always needed people to work for him. He was ever-loyal to the Chief. Subbu could offer countless solutions to the problems of the producer of a film. The narrator comments that film making was quite simple with a man like Subbu around.

Subbu; the Poet

Although he was capable of writing on intricate topics, he wrote poetry for the masses. His success in films overshadowed his literary genius. He composed 'story poems' in folk refrain and diction. He recreated the mood and manner of the Devadasis of the early 20th century.

Subbu; the Actor and the Sycophant

The narrator mocks Subbu by saying that he was an amazing actor. Although he played minor roles, he performed them better than the lead actors. He always said nice things about everything and everyone. His house was crowded with acquaintances and relatives who stayed there permanently. He was really close and intimate with the Boss and so had many enemies.

The Lawyer in the Story Department of Gemini Studios

The Story Department comprised of a lawyer and a group of writers and poets besides Subbu. The lawyer was the legal adviser but everybody referred to him as the illegal adviser! He had unintentionally brought about a sad end to the career of a budding talented actress by recording her outburst against the producer. The legal adviser looked different from the other members of his department as he wore pants and tie while they wore khadi dhotis and white khadi shirts. He was close to the Boss and was allowed to produce a film which flopped. The lawyer lost his job when the Boss closed the Story Department.

Gemini Studios: The Favorite Haunt of Intelligentsia

Gemini Studios was a hot favorite among the poets of that time. It has an excellent mess which supplied good coffee almost round the clock. Those were the days when the Congress government had implemented prohibition and people enjoyed their leisure time over a cup of coffee. Almost everybody seemed to have ample leisure time at the studio.

The Political Ideology at the Studio

Most of the people at the studio wore khadi and greatly appreciated Gandhiji. All of them were opposed to Communism and had many misconceptions about it. They thought Communists to be violent with no filial or conjugal feelings.

Studio Hosts Frank Buchman's MRA (Moral Re-armament Army)

The MRA, a counter-movement to international Communism, visited Madras in 1952. It comprised of 200 people. The narrator had information that the big bosses of Madras played into their hands. The group was criticized by calling it an international circus. The MRA presented two plays, "Jotham Valley' and 'The Forgotten Factor'. Their sets and costumes were wonderful. The Gemini family comprising of six hundred members saw the plays repeatedly. The Tamil and Madras drama community were really impressed by them. The sunrise and sunset scenes of 'Jotham Valley were reproduced in almost all Tamil plays in a similar fashion as that play. The narrator feels that hosting the group was a welcome change from their monotonous routine at the studio.

Another Visitor at Gemini Studios

Another visitor was soon going to visit the Gemini Studios. The staff did not have the faintest idea about him. He was rumoured to be a poet or editor. The visitor was not connected with any of the famous British publications. However, the guest arrived and the Boss read out a very long speech that did not have much to say about the visitor. When the guest's turn came to address the audience, his accent could not be understood by anybody. His visit remained an "unexplained mystery."

A Short Story Contest Organized by 'The Encounter'

The narrator wanted to have an idea about the periodical's credentials before participating in the contest and spending on the postage. He checked at the British Council Library and found out that the editor's name was Stephen Spender. He recalled that this was the same editor who was a guest at the Gemini Studios. The writer felt that he had discovered a long lost brother and immediately sent his entry excitedly.

The Narrator Buys a Low-Priced book 'The God That Failed'

Some years after leaving his job at the Gemini Studios, the narrator bought a low-priced copy of a book 'The God That Failed' released on the 50th anniversary of the Russian Revolution. It was a compilation of six essays by six different authors on their journey into Communism and their disappointed return. Stephen Spender was one of the contributors. The narrator instantly recalled Stephen Spender's visit to the Gemini Studios. Thus, the mystery was finally solved.

Question/Answer

Q1. What does the writer mean by 'the fiery misery' of those subjected to make-up?
Ans: The actors in the make-up room were very uncomfortable due to the heat produced by the lights in the make-up room. As a result, this pain is mentioned by the author. Trouble is described as a state of 'flaming misery.'

Q2. What is the example of national integration that the author refers to?
Ans: The make-up branch of Gemini Studios was an example of national integration. This is because people from many areas and religious groups worked together in the same department, according to the author. A Bengali led the department until he was succeeded by a Maharashtrian. A Dharwar Kannadiga, an Andhra, a Madras Indian Christian, an Anglo-Burmese, and local Tamils were among the other aids.

Q3. What work did the 'office boy' do in the Gemini Studios? Why did he join the studios? Why was he disappointed?
Ans: The office boy applies make-up to the players who acted in front of the audience. He mixed his paint in a large pot on crowd shooting days and applied it fast and noisily on the players' faces. He had gone to the studios hoping to become a famous actor,

screenwriter, director, or lyricist. He was dissatisfied because he had failed and remained a 'boy.'

Q4. Why did the author appear to be doing nothing at the studios?
Ans: The author's job entailed cutting out newspaper clippings on a wide range of topics and filing them away. Many of these have to be scribbled by hand. Onlookers saw him simply ripping up newspapers. As a result, he appeared to be doing nothing to them.

Q5. Why was the office boy frustrated? Who did he show his anger on?
Ans: Despite having a nice opening, the office boy was disappointed because he was still only an office boy. He had received a decent education and would also write poetry. His immense writing gift, on the other hand, was being squandered. He vented his rage on Gemini Studios' No. 2 Kothamangalam Subbu.

Summary

Part 1

Background of the Interview

Having a history of over 130 years, different people have varied opinions about the uses, modes and advantages of interviews. Till now, thousands of celebrities have been interviewed. Every educated person is familiar with it. Some people claim that it is a source of truth while others feel that in practice it is an art.

Opinions about Interviews

Many celebrities despise the interview because it is an encroachment on their privacy. It depreciates their personality in a similar manner as depicted in some primitive cultures, where people believed that, if someone takes a photographic portrait of somebody, then one is stealing that person's soul.

VS Naipaul is of the opinion that interviews injure people as they lose a part of themselves. Lewis Carrol, the creator of 'Alice in Wonderland' was said to have a just 'horror of the interviewer' because he thought he would be treated as a celebrity. His refusals for interviews helped him keep his fans, acquaintances and interviewers at bay. This gave him great satisfaction and amusement. Later he would narrate such experiences with aplomb.

Rudyard Kipling, HG Wells and Saul Bellow's Views on Interviews

Rudyard Kipling vehemently condemned interviews. His wife, Caroline, writes in her diary that her husband refused giving interviews because he considered them immoral, a crime and an assault which is worthy of punishment. According to him, interviews were something vile and cowardly. He neither held the interviewee in esteem nor the interviewer. Although Kipling criticised the interview, he had himself interviewed Mark Twain only a few years before this tirade against interviews.

HG Wells, an eminent science fiction writer, frequently gave interviews but, in an interview in 1894, referred to 'the interviewing ordeal'. Forty years after this comment, he interviewed Joseph Stalin, a great Russian revolutionary. Saul Bellow felt that interviewers created so much tension and pressure that he felt suffocated. He describes interviews as 'thumbprints on his windpipe'.

Summing Up the Genre of Interviews

Despite its disadvantages, the interview is an excellent medium of communication. Denis Brian gives an elevated position to the interviewer because of his power and influence over the interviewee. He terms the interview as an expressive medium.

Part 2

The second part of the chapter is an extract from an interview of Umberto Eco, who is being interviewed by Mukund Padmanabhan from 'The Hindu'.

Umberto Eco is a renowned scholar who is known for his ideas on semiotics (the study of signs), literary interpretation and medieval aesthetics. He is also an author who has an array of works ranging from literary fiction, academic texts, essays, children's books and newspaper articles. He rose to prominence with his work 'The Name of the Rose' which sold a staggering 10 million copies.

Eco's Views on his Philosophical Interests and 'Interstices'

The interviewer, Mukund Padmanabhan, quotes David Lodge (an English novelist) who had expressed astonishment at Umberto Eco's varied and sizeable works. He expresses his surprise by saying that how could one man do all the things that Umberto Eco did. Umberto Eco says that this is a delusive impression about him because he has always been doing the same thing by writing the same philosophical and ethical ideas in different genres.

Eco discloses his secret of producing such voluminous works. He utilises the 'empty spaces' i.e., the shortest gaps between two different works. That's the reason why he has produced so many works. He calls the 'empty spaces' "interstices".

Eco's Intimate and Playful Style

The interviewer questions him about his personalized style of writing which is quite different from the dull and drab style adopted for writing academic works. He asks him if this comes naturally to him or whether he has to make a conscious effort to develop this style.

At this, Umberto Eco replies that he learnt this style of writing when he was 22 years of age. At that time he had presented his first Doctoral dissertation in Italy. His professor was impressed because he had included his trials and errors in it. He had told the story of his research. His Professor published his dissertation as a book which was his way of complimenting his student. Eco understood that he had to adopt the narrative style in his works also. This led him to become a novelist at the ripe age of 50.

At this stage, Umberto Eco remembers his friend, Roland Barthes. Who was, an essayist and died frustrated because he could not fulfil his wish of being a creative writer. Umberto says that he never felt this frustration, as even his essays had a narrative aspect to them. He says that he started writing novels by accident. They catered to his taste for narration.

The Phenomenal Success of 'The Name of the Rose'

One day when Umberto Eco had nothing to do, he tried his hand at writing a novel. "The Name of the Rose' made him famous as a novelist although he is an academician with over 40 works in non-fiction.

Most people know Umberto Eco as a novelist but this doesn't please him. He belongs to the academic community and participates in academic conferences. He writes novels only on Sundays. He accepts the fact that by writing fiction he can reach more people. He says, "I cannot expect to have one million readers with stuff on semiotics".

Mukund, the interviewer, asks him if he is surprised by the staggering success of the novel, 'The Name of the Rose'. As the 'The Name of the Rose' is a serious novel that spins a detective yarn at one level and also ventures into metaphysics, theology and medieval history, it is considered, a difficult and serious read.

Umberto Eco says that he is not puzzled by its staggering sales figures. The only people who look at this in disbelief are journalists and publishers. They believe that people like trash and don't like difficult reading experiences". He applies his own mind to this. He says that after working the whole day he refreshes himself by watching light entertainment programmes such as 'Miami Vice' or 'Emergency Room' after dinner. Similarly, everybody likes light reading only to a certain extent. As such, serious reading does have the capability to draw people.

The medieval period to which this book belongs could have played a major role in its success. For Umberto Eco, the success of the book is a mystery. If he had written it ten years earlier or ten years later it might have not been such a remarkable success story.

Question/Answer

Q1. What are some of the positive views on interviews?
Ans: Interviews are useful means of communication. Almost everybody who is literate reads an interview once in their life. It is a source of truth. In practice, it is an art and varies in its function, methods and merits.

Q2. Why do most celebrity writers despise being interviewed?
Ans: Most of the celebrity writers despise the interview as an unwarranted intrusion into their lives or feel that it somehow diminishes them. They consider themselves as a victim of an interview.

Q3. What is the belief in some primitive cultures about being photographed?

Ans: In many primitive cultures, being photographed is thought to be equivalent to stealing his/her soul and leaving his/her existence incomplete.

Q4. What do you understand by the expression "thumbprints on his windpipe"?
Ans: Celebrity writer Saul Bellow who was interviewed on several occasions expressed it as 'Thumbprints on his windpipe' which means having been muffled. He considers it as an assault on his personality because it creates too much tension.

Q5. Who, in today's world, is our chief source of information about personalities?
Ans: In today's world, the interview has become commonplace in journalism. It is seen as a highly advantageous means of communication. Several thousand celebrities have been interviewed. Through the interview, we got complete and true information. By interacting with other people, we got to know about their experiences, views and feelings.

Chapter - 8   Going Places

Summary

Daydreamer Sophie

Sophie is returning home from school accompanied by her friend Jansie. She tells Jansie that she dreams of owning a boutique after leaving school. Jansie, who is not a dreamer like her, tries to reason that such a thing requires a lot of money.

Sophie replies that she would become a manager till then and save the money needed for the boutique. Jansie again contradicts her childish dreams by saying that she will not be made a manager straight off. Sophie keeps on dreaming about her boutique and says that it will be the best in the city.

Jansie knows that they both are destined to work in the biscuit factory. She is quite practical and is aware of the realities of life. She wishes that Sophie too comes down to reality. But this doesn't bother Sophie, who quite suddenly says that she would then become an actress.

As actresses do not work full time, she would be able to manage her boutique as well. In spite of Jansie's advice that she should not indulge in fantasy, Sophie keeps on babbling about being an actress or a fashion designer.

Sophie's Family also Rubbishes her Dreams

Sophie enters her house talking about money. She belongs to a lower middle class family. Her father retorts by saying that if she ever manages to get some money, she should buy a decent house first. Her little brother Derek mocks her by saying that she thinks money grows on trees. Sophie's mother sighs at her daughter's fantasies.

Sophie notices her mother bending over the sink. Her back has become somewhat bowed with the burden of household work. Their small house is steamy from the stove and dirty dishes are piled up in the corner. Sophie feels a tightening in her throat and goes to look for her brother Geoff.

Sophie is Jealous of Geoff's Silence

Geoff is tinkering with a part of his motorcycle in the next room. He has been out of school for almost three years, and now works as an apprentice mechanic. Sophie ponders over the areas of his life about which he has never spoken.

Geoff is almost a grown-up now and he has developed a habit of speaking less. Sophie is jealous of his silence. Geoff's world remains a fascination for her simply because it is unknown to her. She longs to know him.

She wishes to be admitted more closely into her brother's affections, hoping that someday he might take her along with him to the unknown places in his mind that have so far remained out of her reach. Her father forbids it and she also thinks that Geoff considers her too young. She is impatient to enter the vast unknown world. She dreams of riding behind Geoff on his motorcycle.

Sophie Tells Geoff About her Meeting with Danny Casey

Sophie tells her brother Geoff about her meeting with Danny Casey, an Irish sports star, in the arcade. Geoff is a sports enthusiast and Sophie simply wants to get his attention.

Geoff knows that she is a hopeless dreamer and he doesn't believe her. She says that she met him while window shopping at the Royce. Sophie describes her meeting with Casey. She makes Geoff promise not to tell anybody about the meeting.

Her meeting with Casey was a chance encounter. She wanted his autograph for her younger brother Derek, but neither of them had a paper or pen. Casey and Sophie started talking about the clothes at the Royce's. They decided to meet next week and Casey promised to give her an autograph then.

Geoff doesn't seem to believe her. She gives him details about his physical appearance to make her meeting sound realistic.

Geoff Shares the Story with their Father

Geoff is finally convinced of believing her story and he shares it with their father. Her father's disbelief annoys her, and she adds even more embellishments to her story to make it sound credible. The father and Geoff start discussing about the abilities of Danny Casey. Her father rubbishes Sophie's claims and warns her that one day she will land herself in trouble because of her wild stories.

The Family Goes to Watch the Match

Sophie, Derek and their father sit down near the goal while Geoff, as usual, sits up higher with his friends. United win the match, thanks to the Irish genius, Casey.

Sophie meets Janise and gets surprised by the fact that Janise knows about the meeting with Casey.

She gets angry with Geoff for blurting out her secret. Sophie is worried that if her father gets to know about this, then she will be in trouble. She is relieved to know that Janie has no idea about the date.

Sophie explains to Janise that the meeting was incidental and she doesn't want anybody to know about it. Janise assures Sophie that she can be trusted.

Sophie's Dream is Shattered

Sophie waits for Danny Casey at her favorite spot along the canal. She has always imagined such a perfect date. While waiting, she imagines Casey coming along the river. She tries to strike a balance between her dream world and reality.

The thought of his not coming starts making her sad. Sophie gets miserable at the thought of explaining all this to her family.

Geoff would be disappointed and others would doubt her. She doesn't want to live with the burden of truth. Still she doesn't want to give up her dream.

Sophie Lives her Dream

Sophie once again dreams of meeting Casey at Royce. She asks for an autograph. But they don't have a pen. She imagines his physical appearance. She fails to differentiate her dream from reality. She keeps waiting in the arcade for a long time, remembering Casey's soft melodious voice and the shimmer of his eyes.

As Casey was quite young, Sophie idolized him as her hero. She saw him in a match and, in fact, this was the only time she had seen him.

Question/Answer

Q1. Where was it most likely that the two girls would find work after school?
Ans: Sophie and Jansie would soon pass out of their school. Only a few months were left. Janise knew very well that both of the them were earmarked for biscuit factory. Sophie had wild dreams about her career. Janise was a realist. She knew that they did not pay well for shop work and Sophie's father would not allow her to work there.

Q2. What were the options that Sophie was dreaming of? Why does Janise discourage her from having such dreams?
Ans: Sophie wanted to open a boutique. It would be the most amazing shop that city had ever seen. Alternatively, she would become an actress and have the boutique as a side business. She also thought of being a fashion designer. Janise had her feet firmly planted to the ground. She wanted Sophie to be sensible and drop all her utopian plans because all of them required much money and experience.

Q3. Does Geoff believe what Sophie says about her meeting with Danny Casey?
Ans: No, Geoff doesn't believe what Sophie says about her meeting with Danny Casey. First, he looks round in disbelief and says, "It can't be true". Again he says, "I don't believe it." Sophie then narrates how Danny Casey came and stood beside her. Geoff asks her, "What does he look like?" So, he doesn't seem to be convinced that Sophie met Danny Casey.

Q4. Does her father believe her story?
Ans: No, Sophie's father does not believe her story. When Geoff tells him that Sophie met Danny Casey, his father looked at SopMe with disdain. He ignores her totally. He thinks that it is yet another 'wild story'. He begins to talk about Tom Finny, another great football player.

Q5. How does Sophie include her brother Geoff in her fantasy of her future?
Ans: Geoff was always the first to share her secrets. So, she told him about meeting Danny Casey. She also told him about her plan to meet him next week. She suspected areas of his life about wMch she knew nothing. She longed to know them. She wished that someday he might take her with him. She saw herself riding there behind Geoff.

Flamingo (Poetry)

Chapter -1 My Mother at Sixty-Six

Summary

"Driving from my parent's
home to Cochin last Friday
morning, I saw my mother, beside me,
doze, open mouthed, her face ashen like that of a corpse"

Explanation: The poet had gone to visit her parents' home near Cochin. On Friday morning, she was returning. On her way to the airport, she noticed her mother sleeping beside her in the car. Her mouth was open. Her face was pale and lifeless, just like a dead body. It perhaps expressed the pain she felt because of separation from her daughter.

"And realized with pain that she was as
old as she looked but soon put that thought away
and looked out at young Trees sprinting,
the merry children spilling out of their homes"

Explanation: The poet was alarmed by the sudden realization that old age had crept upon her mother. It was a reality she found hard to accept. The poet was pained to see her mother's colorless pale face. To take her attention away from the disturbing thought, she looked outside the car.

Because the car was moving, the young green trees appeared to be running in the opposite direction. She also saw a group of children rushing out of their homes to play.

All this probably reminded her of her childhood when her mother was young. The young sprinting trees represented how fast time had flown by. The children represented youth, which was full of life and energy. Both the young trees and the children presented a sharp contrast to the mother sitting beside her who was old and suffering from ill-health.

"But after the airport's
security check, standing a few yards
away, I looked again at her, wan, pale
as a late winter's moon"

Explanation: The young children and trees were able to divert her thoughts away. But after reaching the airport and passing through security check, the poet again looked at her mother, who was standing a few yards away from her. Her mother looked lifeless and dull like a late winter's moon, which cannot be seen clearly because of mist and fog.

"And felt that old
familiar ache, my childhood's fear,
but all I said was, see you soon, Amma,
all I did was smile and smile and smile ..."

Explanation: Once again, she was pained to see her mother in this condition. As she was going away and leaving her mother, her old familiar pain, her childhood fear that she

would lose her mother, suddenly came back to her. So she tried to hide her emotions behind her smile. She did not want to reveal her feelings to her old mother and bade her farewell with a smile. She gave hope to her mother and herself by saying that they would meet again and kept on smiling.

Question/Answer

Q1. What is the kind of pain and ache that the poet feels?
Ans: When the poet sees the pale and corpse-like face of her mother, her old familiar pain or the ache returns. Perhaps she has entertained this fear since her childhood. Ageing is a natural process. Time and ageing spare none. Time and ageing have not spared the poet's mother and may not spare her as well. With this ageing, separation and death become inevitable.

Q2. Why are the young trees described as 'sprinting'?

Ans: The poet is driving to the Cochin airport. When she looks outside, the young trees seem to be walking past them. With the speed of the car they seem to be running fast or sprinting. The poet presents a contrast—her 'dozing' old mother and the 'sprinting' young trees.

Q3. Why has the poet brought in the image of the merry children 'spilling out of their homes' ?

Ans: The poet has brought in the image of merry children 'spilling out of their homes' to present a contrast. The merry children coming out of their homes in large numbers present an image of happiness and spontaneous overflow of life. This image is in stark contrast to the 'dozing' old mother, whose 'ashen' face looks lifeless and pale like a corpse. She is an image of ageing, decay and passivity. The contrast of the two images enhances the poetic effect.

Q4. Why has the mother been compared to the 'late winter's moon' ?

Ans: The poet's mother is sixty-six years old. Her shrunken 'ashen' face resembles a corpse. She has lost her shine and strength of youth. Similarly the late winter's moon looks hazy and obscure. It too lacks shine and strength. The comparison is quite natural and appropriate. The simile used here is apt as well as effective.

Q5. What do the parting words of the poet and her smile signify?

Ans: The poet's parting words of assurance and her smiles provide a stark contrast to the old familiar ache or fear of the childhood. Her words and smiles are a deliberate attempt to hide her real feelings. The parting words: "See you soon, Amma" give an assurance to the old lady whose 'ashen face' looks like a corpse. Similarly, her continuous smiles are an attempt to overcome the ache and fear inside her heart.

Summary

"Now we will count to twelve
and we will all keep still.
For once on the face of the Earth
let's not speak in any language,
let's stop for one second,
and not move our arms so much."

Explanation: The poet urges each one of us to count upto twelve and then be quiet. The poet might have used the phrase 'count to twelve as there are 12 hours represented on a clock or as there are twelve months in a year. He might have wanted the people to keep still as long as they could. He wants a moment of silence on the Earth when no language is spoken. In this way, there will be no language barrier between people. No harsh words will be spoken. In this moment of silence, the poet doesn't want anyone to move their arms. He wants us to remain motionless.

"It would be an exotic moment
without rush, without engines,
we would all be together
in a sudden strangeness."

Explanation: The poet feels that such a moment of silence would be an unusual and exciting one. It will have miraculous consequences. There will be no hurry or the sound of machines to pollute the atmosphere. It will be a strange and unfamiliar moment with stillness all around. In this unusual period, the bonds of humanity will get stronger.

"Fishermen in the cold sea would not harm whales
and the man gathering salt would look at his hurt hands."

Explanation: In this moment of inactivity, the fisherman would not be catching fish. Hence, the whales in the sea will be safe. This idea is suggestive of the thought that human beings would not destroy nature. The man who gathers salt will be able to tend to his wounded hands for which he had no time earlier. Thus, both nature and humans will be able to recover from their wounds.

"Those who prepare green wars,
wars with gas, wars with fire,
victory with no survivors,
would put on clean clothes
and walk about with their brothers
in the shade, doing nothing."

Explanation: The poet now speaks of those who wage wars against humanity or environment, wars of all kinds, including the use of chemicals or poisonous gases, wars that bring death and destruction, wars that leave none to celebrate victory. He says that such men should stop their activity shed their clothes stained with the blood of humanity, put on new clothes and walk with their brothers, building brotherhood. The poet implies that the war-torn world should be replaced by one with an atmosphere of peace, brotherhood and harmony.

"What I want should not be confused
with total inactivity.
Life is what it is about;
I want no truck with death."

Explanation: The poet makes a clarification that though he is advocating the need for silence, his advice should not be confused with total inactivity. He does not want any association with death. He says that life is meant to be lived.

"If we were not so single-minded
about keeping our lives moving,
and for once could do nothing,
perhaps a huge silence
might interrupt this sadness
of never understanding ourselves

and of threatening ourselves with death."

Explanation: The poet further advises that people should stop being self-centered and selfish. For one moment they should not think of keeping their lives moving, meeting their ends or fulfilling their duties. That huge silence, which will arise from such a moment, will only serve to help the people. It will help them introspect and overcome their sadness of failing to understand themselves. People have been threatening themselves with death by their activities. This moment of silence will give them time to understand themselves better.

> "Perhaps the Earth can teach us
> as when everything seems dead
> and later proves to be alive.
> Now I'll count up to twelve
> and you keep quiet and I will go."

Explanation: The poet feels that the Earth can enlighten us and guide us in this process of keeping quiet. He wants us to observe that there is some activity under apparent stillness; for instance, a seed appears to be dead', but huge fruit-bearing trees are born' from such seeds lying 'dead here and there.
Finally, the poet thinks that he has said what he intended to. Now he wants us to keep quiet while he is counting to twelve, after which he will leave.

Question/Answer

Q1. What will counting up to twelve and keeping still help us achieve?
Ans: Counting up to twelve takes very short time. Keeping still for this brief interval of time gives us a momentary pause to introspect and review the course of action. It is generally observed that most of the ills and troubles of the world are caused by our rush or hurry. Violence is caused by anger. Keeping quiet and still will give us necessary respite and ensure peace.

Q2. Do you think the poet advocates total inactivity and death?
Ans: No, he doesn't advocate either total inactivity or death. He makes it quite clear that 'stillness' should not be confused with "total inactivity or equated to it. Total inactivity brings death. But Neruda has 'no truck with death'. His stillness means halting of harmful and hostile human activities.

Q3. What is the 'sadness' that the poet refers to in the poem?
Ans: Man's sadness is formed out of his own actions and thoughts. It is quite ironical that man who understands so much fails to understand himself and his action. Rash actions prove harmful and disastrous. Man is the creator of all disasters. He is always threatening himself with death because of his thoughts and actions. This is the tragedy of his life.

Q4. What symbol from Nature does the poet invoke to say that there can be life under apparent stillness?
Ans: The poet wants to prove that there can be life under apparent stillness. The poet invokes the earth as a living symbol to prove his point. The earth never attains total inactivity. Nature remains at work all the time even under apparent stillness. It keeps earth alive. This idea is beautifully illustrated by the following lines: "as when everything seems dead and later proves to he alive."

Q5. Why does Pablo Neruda urge us to keep still?
Ans: Stillness is essential for calm reflection and quiet introspection. We hear the voice of conscience in moments of silence. The poet is convinced that most of human ills and miseries are caused by man's hurry and rush to do things. The poet wishes that we may withdraw ourselves from our undesirable actions and keep still for a moment.

Chapter - 3   A Thing of Beauty

Summary

"A thing of beauty is a joy forever
Its loveliness increases, it will never
Pass into nothingness; but will keep
A bower quiet for us, and a sleep
Full of sweet dreams, and health, and quiet breathing."

Explanation: The poet speaks of the permanent nature of beautiful things which give us eternal joy. Their loveliness keeps on increasing and never fades away. The everlasting beautiful sight of beautiful things is stored in our memory. They give us peace, just like a quiet shady place gives us a sleep full of sweet dreams. A sound sleep results in the good health of our body and mind, as it provides us tranquility and mental peace.

"Therefore, on every morrow, are we wreathing
A flowery band to bind us to the Earth,
Spite of despondence, of the in human dearth
Of noble natures, of the gloomy days,
Of all the unhealthy and o'er-darkened ways
Made for our searching: yes, inspite of all,
Some shape of beauty moves away the pall
From our dark spirits."

Explanation: When we wake up the next morning after a sound sleep, all the beautiful memories of our sweet dreams help us to strengthen our bond with Earth. That is why the poet feels that every morning we prepare a wreath of flowers that binds us to Earth more strongly.

Hopelessness, sadness and lack of noble ways are a part of human life. Life is full of trials and tribulations, lost faith and disappointments, which result from our own doings. We harm ourselves by following unhealthy and wicked paths. But inspite of all this, some wonderful sights of nature help us to shed sad and grim thoughts. They remove the veil of gloom, bringing about hope and optimism in our lives.

"Such the sun, the moon,
Trees old, and young, sprouting a shady boon
For simple sheep; and such are daffodils
With the green world they live in; and clear rills
That for themselves a cooling covert make
'Gains the hot season; the mid forest brake,
Rich with a sprinkling of fair musk-rose blooms;"

Explanation: The poet now goes on to list these objects of beauty. He says that the sun, the moon, old and young trees which provide shade to sheep, the daffodils, the greenery surrounding them, the cool and clear streams which provide respite in the heat of summer and the bushes growing in the forest with musk-roses blooming amidst them, are all eternal sources of joy and pleasure.

"And such too is the grandeur of the dooms
We have imagined for the mighty dead;
All lovely tales that we have heard or read;
An endless fountain of immortal drink,
Pouring unto us from the heaven's brink."

Explanation: The poet adds on further to his list. According to him, there is beauty even in death. He finds beauty in imaginary stories people have made about our dead ancestors who were deemed as heroic and mighty. The poet goes on to say that all the lovely tales that we have heard can also be placed among such things of beauty, as they have a sublime effect on the human spirit. All beautiful things are like an endless fountain from the heavens, sent by God himself, so that mankind may enjoy these precious gifts.

Q1. List the things of beauty mentioned in the poem.
Ans: Everything of nature is a thing of beauty and a source of pleasure. Some of them are: the sun, the moon, old and young trees, daffodil flowers, small streams with clear water, mass of ferns and the blooming musk-roses. All of them are things of beauty. They are a constant source of joy and pleasure.

Q2. List the things that cause suffering and pain.
Ans: There are many things that cause us suffering and pain. Malice and disappointment are "the biggest source of our suffering. Another one is the lack of noble qualities. Our unhealthy and evil ways also give birth to so many troubles and sufferings. They dampen our spirits. They act as a pall of sadness on our lives.

Q3. What does the line, 'Therefore are we wreathing a flowery band to bind us to earth' suggest to you?
Ans: Keats is a lover of beauty. He employs his senses to discover beauty. The link of man with nature is eternal. The things of beauty are like wreaths of beautiful flowers. We seem to weave a flowery band everyday. It keeps us attached to the beauties of this earth.

Q4. What makes human beings love life in spite of troubles and sufferings?
Ans: There are many things that bring us troubles and sufferings. They dampen our spirits. However, 'some shape of beauty1 brings love and happiness in our lives in spite of such unpleasant things. A thing of beauty removes the pall of sadness and sufferings. It makes us love life.

Q5. Why is 'grandeur' associated with the 'mighty dead'?
Ans: The mighty dead were very powerful and dominating persons during their own times. Their achievements made them 'mighty' and great. Their noble works dazzle our eyes. We imagine that such mighty dead forefathers will attain more grandeur on the doomsday. Hence 'grandeur' is associated with the 'mighty dead'.

Summary

The little old house was out with a little new shed
In front at the edge of the road where the traffic sped,
A roadside stand that too pathetically pled,
It would not be fair to say for a dole of bread,
But for some of the money, the cash, whose flow supports
The flower of cities from sinking and withering faint.
The polished traffic passed with a mind ahead,
Or if ever aside a moment, then out of sorts
At having the landscape marred with the artless paint
Of signs that with N turned wrong and S turned wrong
Offered for sale wild berries in wooden quarts,
Or crook-necked golden squash with silver warts,
Or beauty rest in a beautiful mountain scene,
You have the money, but if you want to be mean,
Why keep your money (this crossly) and go along.

Explanation: On the roadside there is an old house which has an extended shed. This shed is towards the edge of the road. The owners have made this towards the edge so that the fast-moving vehicles speeding by may notice and stop there to buy the food and refreshments sold there.

This shed made a pitiable sight, it almost seemed as if it was begging for food but that was not so. Rather it was made so that the rich people who passed by the shed in their beautiful cars would stop there and buy something, so that some cash would flow into the hands of the owners, who then would be able to buy some of the things that are sold in the city.

The poor feel that the money the rich spend to adorn their gardens with flowers can be used to better the lot of the less privileged. But, the rich people passed by without paying any attention to the shed. If anyone cared to stop, it was only due to the irritation at the paint and decor in poor taste that was marring the picturesque scenery of the area. Also, the shed had a board on which the word STAND was painted such that the letters S and N in it were written in reverse, displaying the carelessness of the local people. This shed sold wild berries in wooden boxes and gourds with twisted necks and silver lumps on them

Besides these things, the place also offered a stay in the scenic surroundings. However, the travelers felt that these poorly kept stands spoiled the pristine beauty of the landscape. The rich who passed by the place had the money but had no desire to spend it. According to them, people who looked after the roadside stand were mean and miserly. They wanted to keep the money with them.

The hurt to the scenery wouldn't be my complaint
So much as the trusting sorrow of what is unsaid:
Here far from the city we make our roadside stand
And ask for some city money to feel in hand to try if it will not make our being expand, And give us the life of the moving-pictures' promise
That the party in power is said to be keeping from us.

Explanation: The poet does not want to accuse the rustics of marring the beauty of the landscape. He is more worried about the untold pain that unsaid words cause to the faith of the people belonging to the countryside. The rustics have installed a roadside stand so far away in the countryside just to earn some hard cash.

They long to have a comfortable lifestyle as depicted in movies. They hope against hope that the city citizens may fulfil the promise of giving them economic independence although it was within the purview of the party in power to do so.

It is in the news that all these pitiful kin Are to be bought out and mercifully gathered in To live in villages, next to the theatre and the store,

Where they won't have to think for themselves anymore,
While greedy good-doers, beneficent beasts of prey,
Swarm over their lives enforcing benefits
That are calculated to soothe them out of their wits,

And by teaching them how to sleep they sleep all day,
Destroy their sleeping at night the ancient way.

Explanation: It is in the news that these countryside folk are to be relocated in the villages where they will have all comforts. They will enjoy privileges of the theatre and the local store just like their urban counterparts So busy will be these people in enjoying these comforts that they will have no time to think about themselves or fight for their rights. The 'haves' are called 'beasts of prey' because, in the garb of benefits that they will provide to the rustics, they will exploit them no end. Later the privileged ones will easily forget their promises they made, leaving these poor people more impoverished.

Sometimes I feel myself I can hardly bear
The thought of so much childish longing in vain,
The sadness that lurks near the open window there,
That waits all day in almost open prayer
For the squeal of brakes, the sound of a stopping car,
Of all the thousand selfish cars that pass, Just one to inquire what a farmer's prices are.
And one did stop, but only to plow up grass
In using the yard to back and turn around;
And another to ask the way to where it was bound;
And another to ask could they sell it a gallon of gas
They couldn't (this crossly); they had none, didn't it see?

Explanation: The poet is very disturbed and feels very helpless when he sees their childish longing for money which is never fulfilled. These people keep their windows open all day as if in prayer waiting desperately and uselessly for someone to stop at the stand. Sadness at their disappointment can be noticed all around the place when no one stops there. Out of thousands of cars passing by. just one stopped only to inquire the prices of things sold there. Another stopped just to use the backyard of the place to reverse their car. Yet another stopped just to inquire about the directions for where it wanted to go. The fourth stopped to knew if they could sell them a gallon of gas (petrol). The farmer grumbles in an angry manner that they could see for themselves that it was not sold there. Actually, the country people are upset over the callous attitude of city dwellers. Moreover, it shows the contrast between the thinking of the city denizens and the stark reality of the rural people.

No, in country money, the country scale of gain,
The requisite lift of spirit has never been found,
Or so the voice of the country seems to complain,
I can't help owning the great relief it would be
To put these people at one stroke out of their pain.
And then next day as I come back into the sane,
I wonder how I should like you to come to me
And offer to put me gently out of my pain

Explanation: Finally the poet bemoans that the spirit to scale new heights to break the shackles of economic dependency is not present in the rustics. That is why they do not stop complaining against the economic inequalities. The poet strongly feels that the countryside people should be freed from the pain of poverty and deprivation. Next morning when the poet gains his senses, he wonders what if someone else thinks in the same manner for him so that he is gently relieved from his pain and agony of seeing the miserable condition of these people.

Question/Answer

Q1. The city folk who drove through the countryside hardly paid any heed to the roadside stand or to the people who ran it. If at all they did, it was to complain. Which lines bring this out? What was their complaint about?
Ans: "The polished traffic passed with a mind ahead,
Or if ever aside a moment, then out of sorts
At having the landscape marred with the artless paint
Of signs that with N turned wrong and S turned wrong"
According to the city folk, these stalls with inartistic signboards blemish the scenic beauty of the landscape.

Q2. What was the plea of the folk who had put up the roadside stand?
Ans: The rural folks pleaded pathetically for some customers to stop by and buy some of their goods. City folks used to pass by on this road and hence the rural folk set up the roadside

Q3. The government and other social service agencies appear to help the poor rural people, but actually do them no good. Pick out the words and phrases that the poet uses to show their double standards.

Ans: The poet criticizes the double standards of the government and other social service agencies who promise to improve the standard of living of the poor farmers and show them the rosy side of life. Yet, when the time comes to deliver their promise, they either forget them or fulfill them keeping in view their own benefits. The poet calls them "greedy good-doers" and "beneficent beasts of prey", who "swarm over their lives". The poet says that these greedy people make calculated and well thought-out shrewd moves, to which the innocent, unaware farmers fall prey. These humble and simple farmers are robbed of their peace of mind by these clever people. The poet says, "…..enforcing benefits
That are calculated to soothe them out of their wits,
And by teaching them how to sleep they sleep all day,
Destroy their sleeping at night the ancient way."

Q4. What is the 'childish longing' that the poet refers to? Why is it 'vain'?

Ans: The poet thinks that the persons who are running the roadside stand, suffer from a childish longing. They are always expecting customers and waiting for their prospective customers. They keep their windows open to attract them. They become sad when no one turns up. They are always waiting to hear the squeal of brakes, the sound of a stopping car. But all their efforts go in vain.

Q5. Which lines tell us about the insufferable pain that the poet feels at the thought of the plight of the rural poor?

Ans: Filled with empathy, the poet is unable to bear the plight of the unassuming and innocent rural people. The lines below show his insufferable pain: "Sometimes I feel myself I can hardly bear
The thought of so much childish longing in vain,
The sadness that lurks near the open window there,
That waits all day in almost open prayer"

Chapter - 5 Aunt Jennifer's Tigers

Summary

"Aunt Jennifer's tigers prance across a screen,
Bright topaz denizens of a world of green.
They do not fear the men beneath the tree;
They pace in sleek chivalric certainty."

Explanation: Aunt Jennifer's tigers prance and move across a screen or panel. The poet describes them as bright-coloured like the shining golden-yellow jewel topaz free inhabitants of the green forests, and are not scared of the men standing under the tree. These tigers move about with grace, elegance and confidence. Aunt Jennifer's tigers are not real or living tigers. They are images created by her on tapestry. Aunt Jennifer, who is held captive by the oppressive hand of a patriarchal society, creates in her art an alternate world of freedom. The tigers represent her dreams, her desire to be free from constant fear and oppression that govern her life These majestic and fearless tigers also present a sharp contrast to Aunt Jennifer herself, who is bound by the constraints of married life.

"Aunt Jennifer's fingers fluttering through her wool;
Find even the ivory needle hard to pull.
The massive weight of Uncle's wedding band;
Sits heavily upon Aunt Jennifer's hand."

Explanation: In the second stanza, Aunt Jennifer appears to be creating beautiful images of the tigers by using wool. But she finds it quite hard to pull even the ivory needle. She is so terrorized and tortured that she is unable to carry the weight of the wool. Her fingers flutter. The uncle's wedding band seems heavy on her hand. It suggests that she feels burdened with her marital responsibilities.
Through this stanza, the poet wants to convey the fact that a woman throughout her lifetime works to glorify the tiger', i.e., her husband, but she feels so much subjugated that the marital bond becomes a burden on her. This is also the reality of Aunt Jennifer's life.

"When Aunt is dead, her terrified hands will lie
Still ringed with ordeals she was mastered by.
The tigers in the panel that she made
Will go on prancing, proud and unafraid."

Explanation: The final stanza reveals a sad truth. The poet says that even death will not be able to release Aunt Jennifer from the trauma she had to undergo during her lifetime. Her life will be a story of her ordeals and the oppression that she was subjected to. However, the tigers created by her will be eternal. They will always be proud and unafraid." Here we get a glimpse of an oft-quoted conventional theme in poetry that art endures beyond human life.

Perhaps the poet wants to say that the women themselves are creating these tigers. They need to break their shackles and be unafraid like the tigers themselves. One more thing that can be inferred from the poem is that Aunt Jennifer, who for long has borne the miseries she was subjected to, now longs for freedom from dominance and male chauvinism.

Question/Answer

Q1. Name the poem and the poet of these lines.
Ans: The poem is Aunt Jennifer's Tigers. The poet is Adrienne Rich.

Q2. What are Aunt Jennifer's tigers doing? How do they look like?
Ans: They are jumping across a screen or a wall. They look like shining yellow topaz.

Q3. How was she pulling the needle?
Ans: She was finding even the ivory needle hard to pull.

Q4. How do 'denizens' and 'chivalric' add to our understanding of the tiger's attitudes?

Ans: Like all beasts of prey, the tigers are the denizens of the forest. They live far away from human settlements. They are called 'chivalric.' This indicates the majestic and honorable position that they occupy in the world of animals. So, the use of the words 'denizens' and 'chivalric' adds to our understanding of the tiger's attitudes.

Q5. Why do you think Aunt Jennifer's hands are 'fluttering through her wool' in the second stanza? Why is she finding the needle so hard to pull?

Ans: Aunt Jennifer is weaving tigers on the panel. Her hands are moving about her wool. She is finding the needle quite hard to pull. The weight of years of her married life is lying heavy on her hand. This makes the pulling of the needle so hard.

Flamingo (Vistas)

Chapter-1   The Third Level

Summary

Three Levels at the Grand Central Railway Station

The narrator feels that there are three levels at the Grand Central Railway Station. In reality, there are only two. He has discussed this with his psychiatrist friend, Sam Weiner. Sam feels that the narrator's experience is a waking-dream wish fulfilment. The psychiatrist says that he (the narrator) is unhappy, and the modern man is engulfed in insecurities and fears. So, man wants an escape from his stressful life.

Narrator's Hobby of Stamp Collection; A Refuge

The narrator's psychiatrist friend says that the narrator's hobby of stamp collection is a 'temporary refuge from reality.' The narrator does not agree with this interpretation. He argues that his grandfather lived in 'nice and peacefull times and if this was the case his grandfather did not need to run away from reality. Still his grandfather pursued philately (the collection and study of postage stamps).

Charley Reaches 'The Third Level

One summer night Charley worked late at the office. In a hurry to get back home, he decided to take the subway from Grand Central. He crossed the arched doorway heading for the subway and got lost. The narrator strongly feels that the Grand Central grows like a tree and pushes out new corridors and stairs like roots. The narrator walks down a corridor. He finds nobody but hears empty sound of his own footsteps. He found himself at the third level at Grand Central Station!

Scenario at 'The Third Level

There were smaller rooms, fewer ticket windows and open-flame gaslights there. The information booth was made of wood and looked ancient. Everybody at the station was dressed in the fashion of the late 19th century. To be sure, the narrator got a copy of 'The World' dated June 11, 1989, where the lead story was about President Cleveland.

The narrator goes to the ticket window and demands two tickets for Galesburg, Illinois. He wants to go there with his wife, Louisa. He imagines it to be peaceful countryside in the year 1894 when the First World War was twenty years away and the Second World War was forty years away. To his surprise, the clerk at the ticket counter does not accept his currency bills. Sensing trouble, the narrator runs away from the third level to escape jail.

Charley Buys Old Currency

The narrator withdraws three hundred dollars from the bank next day to buy the currency of 1890. His psychiarist friend is really worried over this. However, his three hundred dollars got reduced to two hundred in old-style bills. He doesn't care because he desperately wants to reach the third level.

Quest for 'The Third Level

The narrator fails to find the third level again. His wife is very worried and pursues Charley to stop looking for the third level. So, he resumed his hobby of stamp collection. His psychiatrist friend, Sam disappears and the narrator and his wife get proof of the existence of the third level. Now both of them start their futile search for the third level platform. The narrator believes the Sam is now is Galesburg in the year 1894.

The Mystery of First-day Covers

When a new stamp is issued, stamp collectors buy it and affix a new stamp on an envelope. They mail the envelope to themselves on the first day of the sale. The postman gives proof of the date. The envelope is never opened and nothing is written inside it. This is called first day cover.

While finicking with his stamp collection, the narrator finds a strange cover mailed to the narrator's grandfather's address in Galesburg. It has been present there since July 18, 1894. It bears a six cent stamps with the picture of President Garfield. The envelope contains a letter for Charley by his friend Sam. Sam confirms the presence of the third level and advises the narrator to keep looking for it. He says 'It's worth it.

Narrator's Reality Check on Sam

Charley finds out that Sam had bought eight hundred dollars worth of old-style currency. This money was sufficient to set up a hay, feed and grain business which Sam dreamt of Sam is a qualified psychiatrist but cannot go back to his profession in Galesburg of 1894 because the profession of psychiatrist did not exist at that time.

Question/Answer

Q1. What does the third level refer to?
Ans: The third level is the world somewhere between desire or dream and reality. It is a world of fantasy that we create for ourselves and occasionally seek to escape to. Most of the time it is a picture of the simple past of our forefathers, who, we believe were happier. It is an escapist's world which one weaves around to be off the current-day problems, worries, anxieties and tensions.

Q2. Would Charley ever go back to the ticket-counter on the third level to buy tickets to Galesburg for himself and his wife?
Ans: Time travel is a temporary relief that man seeks to escape from the rush of his present existence. It was a world of fantasy that Charley too had created. So, he exchanged all his savings for 1894 currency to buy tickets from the third level to Galesburg, Illinois. However, he could not find the third level again as it did not exist.

Q3. Do you think that the third level was a medium of escape for Charley? Why?
Ans: Life today is full of insecurity, fear and worries and time travel is man's way of escaping from it. Occasionally, man seeks escape into the world of fantasy and his nostalgic memories, the happier • times of the past. Yes, the third level was Charley's medium of escape from the mad rat race of modern times.

Q4. What do you infer from Sam's letter to Charley?
Ans: Sam's letter shows man's pining for the simple, less harassing and a happier era. He too had found respite from the hurry and worry of modern life in time travel. Sam had learnt to transport himself into the time period of his ancestors whose quality of life he considered was better than their present existence.

Q5. Philately helps keep the past alive. Discuss other ways in which this is done. What do you think of the human tendency to constantly move between the past, the present and the future?
Ans: Besides philately, there are numerous other ways to keep the past alive. Collecting historical artefacts, paintings and statues in a museum, collecting and reading books, collecting stamps, first day covers, etc. are all a few ways of revisiting history.

Summary

The Prophecy and Miracle about the Tiger King

The Maharaja of Pratibandapuram is known by many names but is often called 'Tiger King'. The author says that everybody who reads about the Maharaja is tempted to meet him, but unfortunately cannot, because he is already dead. However, his myth continues to fascinate people.

When he was born, the astrologers foretold that he would grow up to be a warrior of warriors and hero of heroes, but one day he would have to meet his death. At that very moment, a miracle took place. The baby prince, who was only ten-days old, began to speak aloud clearly and started questioning the astrologers. The prince first said that it was a commonly known truth that anyone who took birth in this world had to die one day, and no predictions were needed in the matter.

He only wanted to know the manner of his death. The chief astrologer told him that because he was born in the hour of the bull, the reason of his death would be a tiger. The child was not even scared. In fact, he warned the tigers to be on their guard, and beware of him.

The Prince's Childhood and the Killing of the First Tiger

The crown prince grew taller and stronger day by day. His childhood was uneventful as compared to his birth. Like other princes in India, the prince drank the milk of an English cow, was looked after by an English nanny, tutored in English by an Englishman and saw nothing but English films.

He was crowned the king at the age of twenty. The astrologer's prediction slowly reached his ears. He went on a tiger hunt and killed his first tiger. Elated by his feat, he sent for the state astrologer. The astrologer again warned the king that the prophecy was right. He might kill ninety-nine tigers but the hundredth tiger would prove to be fatal for him. If the king would succeed in killing the hundredth tiger, the astrologer promised to cut off his tuft of hair, burn all his astrology books and become an insurance agent.

The Tiger Hunt Begins

The Maharaja banned tiger hunting in his kingdom. A proclamation was issued that if anyone dared to fling so much as a stone at a tiger, all his wealth and property would be confiscated. The king was adamant to prove the prediction wrong and vowed to attend to all other matters only after killing a hundred tigers.

The Maharaja faced many dangers on his quest; the bullet missed its mark, a tiger leapt upon him and he had to fight a beast with his bare hands etc. Each time, it was the Maharaja who won.

The Maharaja Comes in Danger of Losing his Kingdom, Bribes to Save it A high ranking British officer visited Pratibandapuram with a wish to hunt tigers. He was very fond of getting his pictures clicked with his victims. The Maharaja was resolute. He refused permission. He felt that if he relented, other British officers too would turn up with the same request.

Now, he stood in danger of losing his kingdom. After many deliberations with his dewan over the issue, they came up with a plan. Fifty diamond rings were sent to the officer's wife. The Maharaja expected that she would choose one or two rings, but the greedy lady kept the whole lot. The bribe cost him three lakh rupees, but his kingdom was saved.

Scheme to kill the remaining Tigers

The Maharaja's tiger hunts were very successful. Within ten years, he was able to kill seventy tigers. As a result, the tiger population became extinct in Pratibandapuram.

The Maharaja devised a scheme for killing the remaining tigers. He called up the dewan and asked him to find a princess of a royal family in any other native state with a large tiger population. The dewan followed the order and found the right girl' for him. The Maharaja killed five or six tigers each time he visited his father-in-law. He managed to kill ninety-nine tigers and then unfortunately the tigers of his father-in-law's kingdom were all dead. Now, only one tiger remained to be killed.

To Escape the Maharaja's Ire, the Dewan Arranges the Hundredth Tiger

The Maharaja was sunk in gloom as he was unable to find the last tiger. Suddenly, there came the news that a tiger had been seen in a hillside village. The Maharaja was so happy at the news that he announced a three year exemption from all taxes for that village and set out on the hunt at once.

The tiger, it seemed, kept himself hidden. The Maharaja's fury and obstinacy mounted alarmingly. He ordered that the land taxes would be doubled. The dewan tried to warn him that such a measure could prove to be catastrophic.

The Maharaja became more outraged and asked the dewan to resign. The dewan, to save himself, decided to give up the old tiger that had been brought from the People's Park in Madras and kept hidden in his house.

The Last Tiger

The dewan and his wife dragged the old and weak tiger to their car and shoved it into the back seat. After much resistance from the tiger, the exhausted dewan was somehow able to leave the tiger in the forest in which the Maharaja had been hunting.

The Maharaja was delighted to see the hundredth tiger. He took careful aim and shot at the beast. The tiger fell in a crumpled heap. The Maharaja was filled with boundless joy at fulfilling his vow. He ordered the tiger to be brought to the capital in a grand procession. After the Maharaja left, the hunters went to take a close look at the tiger. They were shocked to see that the tiger was still alive. The tiger had actually fainted from the shock of the bullet whizzing past him. They decided not to tell the Maharaja that he had missed his target. They feared losing their jobs. One of the hunters then killed the tiger himself.

The Prophecy Proves to be True

The dead tiger was taken in procession through the town and buried. A tomb was erected over it.
After achieving the feat, the Maharaja turned his attention to his child. It was his third birthday and he wished to give him something special. He went for shopping but couldn't find anything worthy enough. Finally, he spotted a wooden tiger and brought it for his son.

The wooden tiger was carved by an unskilled carpenter. Tiny slivers of wood stood up like quills all over it. One of the slivers pierced the Maharaja's right hand while he was playing with his son. He didn't mind it and pulled it out. The next day, infection spread in his hand. In four days, it developed into a festering sore which spread all over his arm. Three surgeons from Madras operated on him but were unable to save his life. Thus, the hundredth tiger took its revenge.

Question/Answer

Q1. Who is the Tiger King? Why does he get that name?
Ans: The Maharaja of Pratibandapuram was called the Tiger King. At the time of his birth the astrologers declared that the prince would have to die one day. The ten-day-old prince asked the astrologers to reveal the manner of his death. The wise men were baffled at this miracle. The chief astrologer said that his death would come from a tiger. The young prince growled and uttered terrifying words: 'Let tigers beware!' He decided to kill one hundred tigers. He, thus, got the name 'Tiger King'.

Q2. What did the royal infant grow up to be?
Ans: Crown prince Jung Jung Bahadur grew taller and stronger day-by-day. He was brought up by an English nanny and tutored in English by an Englishman. He got the control of his state when he came of age at twenty. He decided to kill tigers. For him it was an act of self-defence, as the astrologers had predicted his death by a tiger

Q3. What will the Maharaja do to find the required number of tigers to kill?
Ans: Within ten years the Maharaja was able to kill seventy tigers. Then the tiger population became extinct in the forests of Pratibandapuram. One day the Maharaja sent for the dewan and asked him if he was aware of the fact that thirty tigers still remained to be shot down by his gun. The dewan shuddered with fear. The Maharaja told him that he had decided to get married. He asked the dewan to draw up statistics of tiger populations in different native states. Then he was to investigate if there was a girl he could marry in the royal family of a state with a large tiger population. This plan was put into practice. The dewan found the right girl from a state which possessed a large number of tigers. The Maharaja killed five or six tigers each time he visited his father-in-law. Thus, he was able to find the required number of tigers to kill. He shot ninety-nine tigers.

Q4. How will the Maharaja prepare himself for the hundredth tiger which was supposed to decide his fate?
Ans: Maharaja's anxiety reached the highest level of excitement when only one tiger remained to be killed. He thought of the hundredth tiger during the day and dreamt of it at night. But tiger farms ran dry even in his father-in-law's kingdom. It became impossible to locate tigers anywhere. If he could kill just that one single beast, the Maharaja would have no fear left. As the late chief astrologer had said that Maharaja should beware of the hundredth tiger. The Maharaja was sunk in gloom. Then came a happy news. In his own state sheep began to disappear frequently from a hillside village. Surely, a tiger was at work. The villagers

ran to inform the Maharaja. The Maharaja announced a three-year exemption from all taxes for that village. He set out on the hunt at once. But the tiger was not easily found. The Maharaja continued camping in the forest and waiting for the tiger.

Q5. What will now happen to the astrologer? Do you think the prophecy was indisputably disproved?
Ans: In order to save his skin, the dewan got an old tiger brought from the People's Park in Madras. It was kept hidden in his house. One midnight with the help of his aged wife, he dragged the tiger to the car and shoved it into the seat. He himself drove the car straight to the forest where the Maharaja was hunting. The dewan hauled the beast out of the car and pushed it down to the ground. Next day, the same old tiger wandered into the Maharaja's presence. The Maharaja was overjoyed. He took careful aim at the beast. The tiger fell down in a crumpled heap. The Maharaja was extremely happy that he had killed the hundredth tiger.

The hunters found that the old tiger was not dead. It had only fainted on hearing the sound of the bullet. They did not want the Maharaja to know this fact and lose their jobs. So one of them shot at it and killed it. The dead tiger was taken in procession through the town and buried there. A tomb was erected over it.

The prophecy was not disproved as the king met his death with the infection caused by the sliver of a wooden tiger. The astrologer was already dead. He could not be punished or rewarded.

Chapter - 3   Journey to The End Of The Earth

Summary

The Story Retold

The Journey to Antarctica Begins

The narrator heads towards Antarctica aboard 'Akademic Shokalskiy, a Russian research vessel with a group of high school students. She reveals that Antarctica is the coldest, driest and windiest continent in the world. She commences her journey from Madras, crosses nine time zones, six checkpoints, three water bodies and many ecospheres to reach her destination. Travelling over hundred hours, she feels relief and wonders about the isolation of the continent and the historic time when India and Antarctica were a part of the same landmass.

Gondwana and the Shaping of the Modern World

The narrator takes the reader back to six hundred and fifty million years. At that time, Antarctica was a part of a giant amalgamated Southern supercontinent called Gondwana.
At that time humans had not arrived. The climate was warm and there was a huge variety of flora and fauna. For around 500 million years Gondwana existed. Eventually the landmass broke up and was forced to separate into countries. This shaped our present globe.

Narrator Wonders at Antarctica; Finds It Blissful

Belonging to a relatively warm country, the narrator who is a South Indian is shocked to be in place where 90% of the Earth's total ice volumes are stored! She feels she's walking into a giant ping-pong ball. There is no human life there and nothing to show that human life exists on this planet. She is surrounded by midges, mites, blue whales and limitless expanse of huge icebergs. The surreal twenty four-hour summer lights and eerie silence that is interrupted only by the breaking of an iceberg, is mind-boggling.

Human Impact on the Environment

Human beings have been on the Earth for about 12000 years. In this short span of time we have changed the face of our environment for worse. We have dominated the Earth by establishing cities and megacities. This has led to encroachment of Mother Nature. We are limiting resources on the planet for other creatures. Burgeoning population has added to our woes. The average global temperature is rising and the blanket of carbon dioxide around the world is increasing.

The Paradox of Climate Change

There are many unanswered questions about climate change and the narrator is alarmed by them.
Will the West Antarctic ice sheet melt entirely?
Will the gulf stream ocean current be disrupted?
Will the world come to on end?
In this debate, Antarctica has a major role to play. This is because as compared to other places it remains relatively 'pristine' and contains half-million-years-old carbon records trapped in its layers of ice. The Earth's past, present and future lies hidden in Antarctica.
'Students on Ice' Programme
This programme aims at studying the ecological processes in Antarctica. The narrator works on this project on board Akademik Shokolskiy, It takes school students on the trip of Antarctica. The visit aims at generating a new awareness and respect for our planet in young, impressionable minds.
The programme has been in operation for six years. It is headed by a Canadian, Geoff Green. Earlier he used to take celebrities, retired rich and curiosity seekers to Antarctica for money. Gradually he got sick of those people who gave nothing to the Earth in return. So, he decided to take school students there. It was his firm belief that young minds could learn and act better about the potential hazards regarding the environment which our Earth faces.
The programme was a success because children could see with their own eyes collasping ice shelves and retreating glaciers. They realised that the threat of global warming was real.

Lessons to be Learnt

The greatest lesson to be learnt is little changes in the environment can have big repercussions. The microscopic phytoplankton are nourishment for marine animals and birds in the region. Any more depletion in the ozone layer will affect the activities of these grasses. This will in turn affect the lives of others in this region and the global carbon cycle. The phytoplankton leads us to conclude that if we take care of small things, the big things can be saved.

A Memorable Walk on the Ocean

The narrator says that the experience of strolling on the ocean at Antarctica was a never-to-be-forgotten incident for all. At 65.55 degrees South of equator, the narrator and the students were told to get down. They put on Gore-Tex ice shoes and Sun glasses. On over 180 metres of salt water, there was one metre thick layer of ice. It was a breathtaking experience to see crabeater seals sitting in the periphery. It was truly a memorable experience for all.

The Difference the Antarctic Trip Made

The author is overwhelmed with the beauty of balance in play on our planet. She has many questions in her mind for e.g., what would happen if Antarctica becomes a warm place? Will human beings survive on Earth? Whatever be the answers to these questions, she is full of optimism about the teenagers who are full of idealism to save the Earth after having made the trip of Antarctica.

Question/Answer

Q1. 'The world's geological history is trapped in Antarctica.' How is the study of this region useful to us?

Ans: Antarctica was once a part of the supercontinent Gondwana land. It later got separated from India and drifted south to create the present continent. The climate on the land changed from warm and humid to extremely cold and frigid. It hence carries a lot of history with itself and can be useful for archaeological purposes too. It is a place one should visit to get a glimpse of past, present, and future coexisting together in a pure and realistic form. The secrets of life are embedded in the deep layers of ice. Antarctica also provides us warning signs to foresee the consequences of present damage to the environment are. It reminds us that the effects of global warming are real and can produce disastrous consequences.

Q2. What are Geoff Green's reasons for including high school students in the Students on Ice expedition?

Ans: Tishani Doshi traveled South to the end of the Earth to Antarctica along with an expedition group 'Students on Ice.' Geoff Green took high schools on the expedition because he wanted to make young minds sensitive about climatic changes that are happening around the world. He believes that these young minds are the future policymakers of the world, and it is in their hands that the future lies. He considers them to be the best ones to shoulder the responsibility to save the world and the environment and can turn the situation better.

Q3. 'Take care of the small things and the big things will take care of themselves.' What is the relevance of this statement in the context of the Antarctic environment?

Ans: The statement points out the fact that building up trivial habits and making insignificant changes can bring a substantial change in the world we live in. If every individual takes small steps, the total impact on the world will be massive. The book provides an example of phytoplankton, which are small photosynthetic plants and serve as food for several marine birds and animals. If the ozone layer depletes further, the phytoplankton might get depleted and its contribution to the ecosystem will be depleted which in turn would affect the globe on a large scale. We need to focus on small things and make slight changes so that we can save the world together and make it a better place to live.

Q4. Why is Antarctica the place to go to, to understand the earth's present, past, and future?

Ans: Antarctica was part of the Gondwana land. It, hence, has a mass of lands that have existed millions of years ago and is untouched by humankind. Its present state of melting and breaking apart tells us about the crisis the environment is going through now. Our neglect of the environment has led to an increase in global warming. The state of earth points out the fact that if the present state continues the earth will not sustain for long and the end is near. We need to be conscious and take small steps to protect our Earth from the potential threat and decline its heading towards.

Q5. How do geological phenomena help us to know about the history of humankind?

Ans: Geographical lands carry fossils as imprints of history. The fossils provide us with major evidential data to study evolutionary history. Using modern technology like Carbon Dating helps us to determine the age of the fossil. Various civilizations have been excavated at various locations across the globe. Mammals and other flora and fauna existed on land even before the separation of landmass.

Chapter - 4   The Enemy

Summary

Dr Sadao Hoki and his Traditional Father

Dr Sadao Hoki, a famous Japanese surgeon and an accomplished scientist, lived in a house on the Japanese coast. The house was set upon rocks above a narrow beach surrounded by pine trees. As a child, Sadao used to climb these trees. He often visited the South Sea islands with his father. His father believed that the islands were stepping stones to Japan's future to gain perfection. Sa ao's father was a very serious and traditional man. He never joked or played with him but took infinite pains for his son. Sadao's education was his chief concern. He even sent Sadao to America to complete his studies. Sadao's father inculcated in him values of patriotism and national loyalty when the latter was quite young and Sadao had always cherished these great virtues.

The Second World War started, but Sadao was not sent with the troops because he was about to make a discovery which would render wounds entirely clean. Also, the Gener' who was old, was being treated by Sadao, and he might require an operation any-time.

Sadao met Hana in America, Waited for his Father's Consent to Marry Her

Sadao had met Hana in America, but he had waited until he was sure that she was Japanese before deciding to marry her. His father would never have approved of her otherwise. Sadao recalled that his meeting with Hana was an accident. Sadao lived in Professor Harley's house and had almost not gone to the Professor's house that night, where he met Hana, a new student.

After Sadao and Hana had finished their studies, they came home to Japan. The marriage was solemnised in the traditional Japanese way according to his father's wishes. They were a happy couple.

The Prisoner is Washed Ashore

One night, Sadao and Hana were enjoying the view of the sea from their verandah when they saw something black coming out of the mists. It was a man. He staggered a few steps and then the mists hid him again. When they saw him again, he was crawling. Sadao thought that he was a fisherman washed ashore from his boat.

The surf beyond the beach was spiked with rocks. The man might be badly hurt. They found the man wounded. Hana realised that it was a white man. The fellow was young and unconscious.

The man was bleeding profusely. Sadao saw that a bullet wound had reopened. Sadao packed the wound with sea moss. The man moaned with pain, but he did not awaken. Sadao wanted to throw the man back into the sea, as he had now realised that he was an American prisoner of war. Hana also agreed. Sadao knew that giving shelter to the enemy would get them into trouble. He was torn between his moral duty as a doctor which urged him to save the dying man and his national duty which required handing him over to the Army as a patriot. Both Hana and Sadao finally decided to take the man home, as he was in need of urgent medical attention.

The Servants React Bitterly

They decided that they should tell the servants also. They would tell them that they intended to hand him over to the police. The man had been starved for a long time and he was light as a fowl. They carried him to Sadao's father's bedroom as his father was no longer alive. The old man had never allowed a foreign object in his room.

The American was very dirty and needed to be washed. Hana said that Yumi, the governess, might wash her. She went to fetch her. When she returned to the kitchen, she found the other two servants frightened at what Sadao had told them. The servants tried to convince Sadao that he must hand over the enemy to the police. Yumi refused to wash the American and Hana had to wash him herself.

Sadao Saves the Enemy's Life

Sadao was ready to operate. He was completely absorbed in his work. He told Hana that she would need to give anaesthetic to the man. Hana probably had never seen an operation and started vomiting. Sadao was irritable and impatient with his enemy, as he was not able to help Hana in her distress. The man groaned with pain.

Interestingly enough, Hana was able to assist her husband in the operation. Hana noticed deep red scars on the neck of their enemy. She wondered if the war torture stories she had heard were actually true. She recalled that General Takima was a ruthless man who didn't even spare his wife.

Sadao murmured while operating, as was his habit. He called the enemy his friend'. Sadao finally succeeded in taking the bullet out. He was sure that the man would live in spite of his sufferings.

The Patient gets Better but the Servants Decide to Leave

Hana took good care of the man. She served him, as the servants refused to enter the room. The man was surprised to see Hana talk in English. Hana told him that she had lived in America for a long time. The enemy revealed his name to Hana. His name was Tom. Sadao was still confused about handing him over to the police.

The servants resented their decision to help the American soldier. Hana told Sadao that the servants would not live in the house if the enemy was still present. The servants thought that the couple liked Americans. Sadao tried to clarify that all Americans were his enemies. They talked about the consequences of harbouring an enemy. Hana could hear what they were talking about. On the seventh day, the servants left.

The General's Messenger; Sadao Goes to See the General

On the same day, a messenger in official uniform came to Sadao's house. Hana was so scared that she was unable to speak. She thought that he was there to arrest Sadao. In fact, the messenger had come to inform Sadao that the General needed him. Looking at Hana in utter distress, Sadao decided to get rid of the man.

Sadao told the whole episode to the General. The General knew that Sadao was indispensible to him. He never trusted other Japanese surgeons. The General promised Sadao that nothing would happen to him.

The General then planned to get the American soldier assassinated. He told Sadao that his private assassins were very competent and would also remove the dead body. Sadao thought that this plan would be the best for his family.

After that meeting, Sadao spent three restless nights waiting for the assassins. But they didn't come. Finally, the torture became too much to bear for him. He planned to get rid of the enemy himself.

Sadao Helps the Enemy

Sadao told the escape plan to Tom. He also warned him that he needed to escape as the news of his presence was not hidden any more. He arranged a boat, food, drinking water and clothing for the young man and also gave him his own flashlight. He told Tom that he should flash the light two times if he needed something, once if everything was fine. He must do this only when the sun dropped under the horizon. He further added that Tom could find many fish to eat but he should eat them raw, lest the fire be seen. Even Hana didn't know about this plan. Sadao had told Tom to wait for a Korean ship.

Sadao went to the General and informed him that the American had escaped. The General informed Sadao that he forgot about the prisoner, as he was unwell. He told Sadao not to leak out this information to anybody. Back at home, Sadao remembered his days in America and the Americans he met there. He wondered why he could not kill Tom, his enemy.

Question/Answer

Q1. Who was Dr. Sadao? Where was his house?
Ans: Dr. Sadao Hoki was a famous yet sympathetic and loyal Japanese scientist and surgeon. He was a grounded man and lived in an ancestral stone house in Japan built above a narrow beach on the coast, outlined by narrow pine trees. He spent about eight years in America to improve his skill and learn everything possible about medicine and surgery. When the chapter begins, we are introduced to his scientific research to discover a drug that would render the wound entirely clean.

Q2. Will Dr. Sadao be arrested on the charge of harbouring an enemy?
Ans: Dr. Sadao stayed loyal to the vows of the medical profession. He saved the injured man, who was washed off on the shore near his home irrespective of him being American. He was aware of the fact that his country and America had political tensions and this step would put the whole family in danger. Still, he went ahead with his duty as a doctor and a human and saved the enemy. So, if we see from a humanitarian perspective, he should not be punished for this, since he did what his profession taught him, and doctors should help humanity irrespective of country and political issues.

Q3. Will Hana help the wounded man and wash him herself?
Ans: Hana will help the wounded man. Though it is difficult for her since she is not medically trained and afraid of him since he was an American, she would try her best. Hana and Sadao are husband and wife. I believe they would share common values and moral values. Both would want to serve and help humanity in one way or the other possible. She tries her best to contribute as much as possible to the noble cause alongside her husband. Even though her act was so impulsive after her servant Yumi defied her orders, she still did it with utmost sincerity.

Q4. What will Dr. Sadao and his wife do with the man?

Ans: Dr. Sadao and his wife would help the man. The man was unconscious and a prisoner of war. He was a great threat to the family but even then, decided to treat and operate on him. It was his responsibility as a doctor to serve humanity and adhere to the vows of his profession. Hana helped to clean the man after Yumi defied to follow the orders to do the same. They fed him and tried their best to create an escape path for him. Even though they knew they would have to hand him over to the army sooner or later, they still provided him the best possible.

Q5. Will Dr. Sadao be arrested on the charge of harbouring an enemy?

Ans: Dr. Sadao could be arrested if someone complained about the family harbouring an enemy in their home. The servants were even worried too when they realized that their master was helping an enemy which would lead them all to prison. They were against this and left the work immediately to save their lives, Hana and Sadao even then, though half-heartedly, still helped the enemy to recover. On humanitarian grounds, the cat was well justified but it was against the political setup of the country. Sadao was close with the General and was treating him for the heart ailment. The chances were slim that the General would risk his own life at the jeopardy of the country's safety.

Chapter - 5 On the Face of It

Summary

The Meeting in the Garden
The first scene of the play begins in Mr Lamb's garden. Derry, a young boy of fourteen, climbs over the garden wall and enters the garden. He walks in slowly and cautiously, thinking nobody is there, but is startled to hear Mr Lamb's voice. The old man tells Derry to not trip up on the crab apples which have fallen from the tree in the garden. Derry tries to explain to him that he didn't want to sneak in. He had presumed that the house was empty, and he didn't expect anybody there. He appears to be scared. Mr Lamb tries to put his fears at rest and says that the house is no doubt empty, now that he is in the garden. Mr Lamb assures him that there is nothing to be afraid of. His gates are always open and everyone is welcome.

Derry Appears to be Apprehensive
When Mr Lamb tells Derry that there is nothing to be afraid of, Derry replies that he is not afraid but people are afraid of him. Derry is very furious because he thinks that Mr Lamb is having pity on him. He vehemently says that he is not a 'poor boy'. He is afraid of himself because one side of his face got burnt, as acid fell on it. Mr Lamb, seeing that the situation has become a bit heated, changes the subject. He says that he is going to make jelly out of the crab apples. However, this enrages Derry more. He tells Mr Lamb that he has changed the subject because he is also afraid of his burnt face, just as all other people are. He says that people pretend to be sympathetic towards him but are afraid to talk about his looks because he was ugly.

Mr Lamb's Philosophy
Mr Lamb tells him to talk about it, but Derry has become upset. The old man says that it is possible Derry's face got burnt in a fire. Derry tells him that it is acid that has burnt his face. He says, "It ate my face up. It ate me up". Derry is confused at Mr Lamb's indifference and asks him if he is not interested. Mr Lamb replies that he is interested in everybody. There is nothing God made that doesn't interest him. He asks Derry why one green plant is called a weed and another a flower. Mr Lamb doesn't find any difference; to him, it's all life. His philosophy is to celebrate life in all its forms.

Mr Lamb Reveals his Impairment
Mr Lamb tells Derry that one of his legs got blown off in a war, but that is not important. When he goes out, some kids call him "Lamey-Lamb". This doesn't bother him. He thinks that such a name suits him. Derry says that Mr Lamb could cover his tin leg with his trousers, and none would notice it or stare. But Derry could not cover his face. According to Mr Lamb, there are plenty of other things in the world which are important. Mr Lamb has a positive and optimistic attitude towards life. He feels that beauty is relative and reminds Derry of 'Beauty and the Beast'.
Derry is filled with bitterness. He says that he doesn't believe in fairy tales. His face will always remain the same. He also says that no one will kiss him, but his mother will kiss him because she has to. She kisses him on the other side of his face.
Mr Lamb tries to reason with him. He says that he should notice the beautiful things in the world and not care about his face. Derry begins to mock the idea, saying that one should think of all those people who are worse off than yourself. This may be true, but it won't change his face.

Derry Calls Mr Lamb Peculiar
Derry narrates an incident which happened at the bus stop. He heard two women talk about his face. One of them said, "Look at that, that's a terrible thing. That's a face only a mother could love." He is very hurt and calls it cruel. Mr Lamb advises him not to believe everything that he hears. To this, Derry replies that he finds Mr Lamb 'peculiar'. He further tells him that he came in the garden because he liked it. But he doesn't like being near people.

Mr Lamb starts telling him a story about a man who was afraid to die. He feared each and every thing and locked himself in a room. Unfortunately, he died because a picture fell off the wall on his head. Derry laughs a lot at the story. Through this story, Mr Lamb wanted to show Derry that one cannot hide oneself or shun society just because of some fear. One should enjoy life as it comes.

The Positive side of Life
Derry notices that there are no curtains on the windows of Mr Lamb's house. Mr Lamb replies that he is not fond of curtains because they shut things out and he likes to see the light and the darkness, and to hear the wind.
Derry also says that he likes to hear the rain falling on the roof. Mr Lamb says that Derry is not lost. It means that there is still a sensitive part in his heart but it is hidden because of the bitterness.

Derry tells Mr Lamb that even his family has pity on him. They think about his future and what will he do with that face. They feel that it would be difficult for him to get on in this world with a face like that. Mr Lamb shows him that he is better than all the rest. He can live his life easily like others do.

Derry asks Mr Lamb if he has any friends. Mr Lamb tells him that everyone is his friend, even Derry. Derry is confused and asks him how they are friends when Mr Lamb doesn't even know his name. Mr Lamb explains that names don't signify anything. To him, being friends doesn't mean that you should know all the details about a person.

At this point, Derry chooses to tell him his name. He says it's Derek, but hates being called that. He wants to be called 'Derry' only. 'Watching, Listening, Thinking'

Derry tells Mr Lamb that he hates some people. Mr Lamb says that hatred is more dangerous than the acid that burned his face. Derry narrates another incident about the time when he returned home after the accident.
He heard someone say that he'd have been better in the hospital with others like him'. Mr Lamb contradicts it by asking what kind of a world would that be. Derry is amazed and asks how he understands all these things. Mr Lamb replies, 'Watching, listening, thinking'.

Mr Lamb tells Derry that he can come and go in his house as he wishes. Whatever belongs to him belongs to everybody. Derry tells Mr Lamb that his friends would run away at seeing Derry's face. Mr Lamb tells him that it is a 'risk' he has to take. He wants Derry to understand that he has to come out of his shell and shed his bitterness if he wants to live life to the fullest.

Derry Offers his Help
Derry asks Mr Lamb how he is going to get the apples down, since his leg is blown off and he wears a tin leg. Mr Lamb assures him that over the years he has learned to deal with his handicap. Derry says that he could help him, but his mother won't allow him to come out once he gets home.

Mr Lamb tells Derry that it is not Derry's mother but Derry's bitterness and hesitation that won't let him go out. Derry tries to give a reason by saying that people worry too much and his house is three miles away. Mr Lamb excites Derry by saying that he is a young boy and he could do anything if he chooses to. The power of choosing what one wants lies in one's own hands. A small altercation takes place between them. Mr Lamb says that Derry doesn't have the guts to fight the odds. His burnt face is just an excuse. Derry becomes infuriated and mocks the tin leg of Mr Lamb. He promises to return to the garden.

Derry Chooses for Himself
The second scene begins in Derry's house. He is fighting with his mother because he wants to return to Mr Lamb, and his mother is not allowing him to go. She says that she has been warned by many people that Mr Lamb appears to be an eccentric. But Derry insists that he wants to go. For the first time in his life, someone has shown him the right way. He wants to talk to Mr Lamb about things which matter to him. He wants to sit there and listen to things. His mother tells him to stay, but Derry tells her that he hates it. His mother doesn't react. She simply tells him that he is bound to say such awful things because of his face. Derry strongly replies that he doesn't care about his face anymore. The transformation has begun.

Derry is a Changed Persons
The final scene shifts to the garden again. Derry reaches there out of breath. He finds Mr Lamb lying on the ground. He has been trying to pick the apples off the tree when the ladder has slipped and he, alongwith it, has fallen on the ground.

Derry tries to awaken him, but Mr Lamb is unmoving. He is probably dead. Derry has lost his only friend and he begins to cry. Mr Lamb was able to do what he has been trying; he has taught Derry how to live.

Question/Answer

Q1. Who is Mr Lamb? How does Derry get into his garden?
Ans: Mr Lamb is an elderly gentleman with a rusted leg. Years ago, during the war, his real leg was blasted off. He is the sole occupant of his home which has a garden. It's filled with luscious crab apples that are orange and golden in colour. When Derry jumps over the garden wall to get into Mr Lamb's garden and does not utilise the open door to enter only to find Mr Lamb sitting in his garden.

Q2. Do you think all this will change Derry's attitude towards Mr Lamb?
Ans: Yes, Derry's attitude toward Mr Lamb will change as a result of all of this. Derry's charred face has made him the target of scorn. People sympathized with him, but it was never a heartfelt sympathy. As a result, he developed a negative outlook on life.

Everyone loathed and despised him, he believed. Mr Lamb, on the other hand, showed no sympathy for him. Mr Lamb had a tin leg, and Derry had a burnt face, so Mr Lamb could sympathize with him. He assisted the youngster in learning to love and live a happy life without disrespect for himself. Derry had initially dismissed the elderly man as ordinary, but he grew to appreciate and admire him as a result of what he said.

Q3. What is it that draws Derry towards Mr Lamb despite himself?
Ans: Mr Lamb is distinct from the others, according to Derry. When Mr Lamb sees Derry's charred face, he exhibits no surprise or alarm. Instead, he speaks to him in a caring tone. He extends a warm welcome to him in his backyard. He offers to help him by picking apples and making jelly. He refers to him as a friend. He claims that things may appear to be different on the surface, but they are all the same on the inside. He uses flowers, trees, plants, and weeds as examples. They may differ in appearance, but they are all growing live organisms. People can have diverse outward appearances, yet they are all the same on the inside. When Mr Lamb hears Derry declare he dislikes some individuals, he says it can injure him more than any bottle of acid. Hatred, on the other hand, burns one's insides - the soul. He encourages Derry to forget about his burned face. He has two arms and legs, as well as eyes, ears, a tongue, and a brain. And if he has a strong mind, he will be able to outperform others. Mr Lamb attracts Derry to himself with such words of encouragement.

Q4. In which section of the play does Mr Lamb display signs of loneliness and disappointment? What are the ways in which Mr Lamb tries to overcome these feelings?
Ans: Although Derry's loneliness is the focus of the play
Mr Lamb's loneliness is evident in the first scene of the play.
He claims to have heard the bees for a long time and that they sing instead of buzz, which shows his perception differs from others and his lack of companionship.
Mr Lamb spent the entire day sitting in the sun reading books, indicating that his only actual friends were books.
He mentions that his empty house is full of books, implying that reading filled the hole in his life.
When he mutters to himself that no one comes back to him after the first meeting, it becomes evident that he is lonely and disappointment.
Mr Lamb does not anticipate Derry's return and ascends the ladder himself to collect all the apples, showing his lack of expectation for companionship.
Ironically, if Derry had not returned, Mr Lamb would have died unnoticed, highlighting the extent of his loneliness.

Q5. The actual pain or inconvenience caused by a physical impairment is often much less than the sense of alienation felt by the person with disabilities. What is the kind of behaviour that the person expects from others?
Ans: If he is not mocked and punished with cold pity, a person with any physical handicap can live a life of dignity and honour. Instead of sympathy, he expects empathy. If everyone looks down on him with a pessimistic attitude, he may never be able to shake his sadness and, as a result, retreat to his little world. He's already under a lot of mental and emotional strain. As a result, he expects others to be understanding rather than point out his handicap. Derry and Mr Lamb are both caught in a similar scenario in the play. Mr Lamb, as an adult, is capable of dealing with such issues, but Derry, as a youngster, is unable to unravel this web on his own. He takes a liking to this elderly man because he said the words to someone who was going through the same humiliation. The old man assumed the child would want to hear him.

Chapter - 6   Memories of Childhood

Summary

i.   The Cutting of My Long Hair

First Day at School

The writer recalls that her first day in the land of apples was bitterly cold, with snow covering the surroundings. Besides, her first experience at the school, where she was admitted with other Native American boys and girls, was equally unpleasant. The noise made by the breakfast bell crashed into her ears. The clatter of shoes and the constant clash of harsh noises were pretty annoying. Zitkala-Sa longed for freedom, but it was useless to think of it.

The Embarrassment

A white woman placed them in the line of girls who were marching into the dining room. The narrator noticed that they were Native American girls, who wore closely clinging dresses and stiff shoes. The small girls wore sleeved aprons and had shingled hair. She was feeling very uncomfortable in the school dress. Besides, her blanket had been taken off from her shoulders, making her feel all the more embarrassed. She found other Native girls more immodestly dressed than her, in their tightly fitting clothes. She also saw boys come in from the opposite door. A small bell was tapped and every student pulled out a chair from under the table. The narrator also pulled out a chair and sat down. But she was surprised to find that she was the only one sitting.

Just as she began to rise, a second bell was rung. All sat down and she had to crawl back into her chair again. She heard a man at one end of the hall and he was praying. The other students sat with their heads hung over their plates.

As the narrator was glancing at the surroundings, she caught the eyes of a paleface (white) woman upon her. She wondered why the woman was looking at her so keenly. After the man ceased his mutterings, a third bell was tapped and everybody started eating with a knife and fork. Zitkala-Sa instead started crying. She probably had never eaten using knives and forks. All the new changes were too much for her to take.

The Terrible Warning

The eating-by-formula was not the end of her woes. Her friend Judewin knew some English, and she had overheard the white woman talk about cutting their long and heavy hair. The thought of having her hair cut was unacceptable to the narrator. Her mother had taught her that only skilled warriors who became prisoners in war had their hair shingled (cut) by the enemy. In their society, short hair was worn by mourners and shingled hair by cowards.

The Narrator's Protest

Judewin thought that the school people were strong and they would all have to allow their hair to be cut, but Zitkala-Sa was ready to put up a fight. She told her friend that she would struggle first, and not submit willingly before the oppressors.

When she got the chance to escape, she crept upstairs unnoticed. She entered a large room. It was dark, as the curtains were drawn. Zitkala-Sa crawled under the bed farthest from the door. After some time, people started searching for her. She heard Judewin call her name, but she didn't answer.

The Cutting of Zitkala-Sa's Hair

Finally, the women and girls who were looking for Zitkala-Sa entered the room in which she was hiding. She held her breath while the others searched the room. The next thing she remembered was being dragged out. She was resisting, kicking and scratching wildly. She was carried downstairs and tied to a chair. At last she felt a cold scissor blade against her neck gnaw off one of her thick braids. This was the end of her resistance. She lost her spirit.

She was reminded of all the humiliations she went through since the day she parted with her mother. She was deeply sad and nobody comforted her. She missed her mother and felt like an animal driven by a herder.

The Entertaining Walk Home

This is the second part of the unit. The narrator takes us back to her childhood when she was a carefree child studying in the third class. The walk from school to home was hardly of 10 minutes. But it would take her half an hour to one hour to cover the distance. The entertaining sights would tie her legs and stop her from going home.

The performing monkey, the snake charmer, the cyclist who kept pedalling for many days, the Maariyaata temple and the pongal offering being cooked outside it were just some of the interesting sights. And then there were other things going on in the market like a political procession, puppet shows and stunt performances. The market was full of seasonal fruits and stalls. The narrator felt spellbound by all the variety.

Encounter with Untouchability

One day, when the narrator was returning home, she saw a threshing-floor set up on her street. A landlord was watching over the proceedings. The people of her caste were driving the cattle. Just then, she noticed an elder of her street. He was carrying a small packet, holding it with a string. It contained some vadai and the packet had become wet. The narrator thought to herself that the packet might come undone, but still the elder was not touching it. The way he walked made Bama shriek with laughter. The elder crouched while handing over the packet to the landlord.

Laughter Turns to Sadness

The narrator returned home and told her elder brother Annan about the incident. She was laughing uncontrollably, but Annan didn't seem to be amused. Annan told her that the elder and they were considered low caste. The landlord belonged to the upper caste. The upper caste people thought that if low caste people touched them or anything that belonged to them, they or it would be polluted'. That's why the elder was carrying the packet by its string. After hearing this, the narrator didn't want to laugh anymore. She felt infuriated and provoked. She wondered how these fellows thought so much of themselves. She felt compelled to touch the wretched vadais herself.

Annan's Advice

Annan told Bama that because they were born into a low caste community, they were never given any honour or dignity or respect. He advised her to study hard and learn all that she could, because only education could help them throw off all the indignities. These words made a deep impression on Bama. She studied hard. As Annan had urged, she stood first in her class and because of that, many people became her friends.

ii. We Too Are Human Beings

The story is written by Bama who is one of the characters in this story. She is a little cheerful girl who loves to observe things taking place in her street. She says though it takes only ten minutes to reach home from her school but she takes about thirty minutes to reach her home from the school. She then explains the reason behind it. She says when she is on her way to home she sees a monkey performing and a snake charmer doing some act with his snake which was very interesting for her. Then there was a cyclist also who was cycling from past three days. There was one famous temple which had a big bell and a tribal man who sells clay beads, needles etc. She also comes across various snack stalls and street acts. Then she explains about how various political parties come to her street to give lectures. As she proceeds further, she saw a landlord sitting and watching his workers work in the field. She then saw an old man of her community handling a snack pack in a very strange manner and then offering it to the landlord. She founds it so amusing that she bursts out into a laugh. On reaching home she narrates it to her elder brother and starts laughing. He then tells her a real truth about her being from a low caste and that the upper caste people do not like their presence or touch the low caste as it would make them impure. She finds it so disgusting that she grows angry over the upper caste people. Some days later her elder brother is questioned about his whereabouts to know his caste. He then suggests her to study hard as only this could earn her respect. She works as per his suggestions and become topper of her class. This not only earns her respect but many friends too.

Question/Answer

Q1. What does Zitkala-Sa remember about her 'first day in the land of apples'?
Ans: It was a bitter-cold day. The snow still covered the ground. The trees were bare. A large bell rang for breakfast. Its loud metallic sound crashed through the belfry overhead and penetrated into their sensitive ears.

Q2. How did Zitkala-Sa react to the various sounds that came when the large bell rang for breakfast?
Ans: The annoying clatter of shoes on bare floors disturbed the peace. There was a constant clash of harsh noises and an undercurrent of many voices murmuring an unknown tongue. All these sounds made a bedlam within which she was securely tied. Her spirit tore itself in struggling for its lost freedom.

Q3. Where were the girls taken and how ?
Ans: The girls were marching into the dining room in a line. The Indian girls were in stiff shoes and tightly sticking dresses. The small girls wore sleeved aprons and shingled hair. They did not seem to care that they were indecently dressed.

Q4. "I felt like sinking to the floor", says Zitkala-Sa. When did she feel so and why ?
Ans: It was her first day at school. She was marching into the dining room with other girls in a line. She walked noiselessly in her soft moccasins. But she felt that she was immodestly dressed, as her blanket had been removed from her shoulders. So, she felt like sinking to the floor.

Q6. How did Zitkala-Sa find the 'eating by formula' a hard trial?

Ans: She did not know what to do when the various bells were tapped and behaved unlike others. When the first bell rang, she pulled out her chair and sat in it. As she saw others standing, she began to rise. She looked shyly around to see how chairs were used. When the second bell was sounded, she had to crawl back into her chair. She looked around when a man was speaking at the end of the hall. She dropped her eyes when she found the paleface woman looking at her. After the third bell, others started eating, but she began to cry.

www.ingramcontent.com/pod-product-compliance
Lightning Source LLC
Chambersburg PA
CBHW060124120726
48003CB00009B/2770